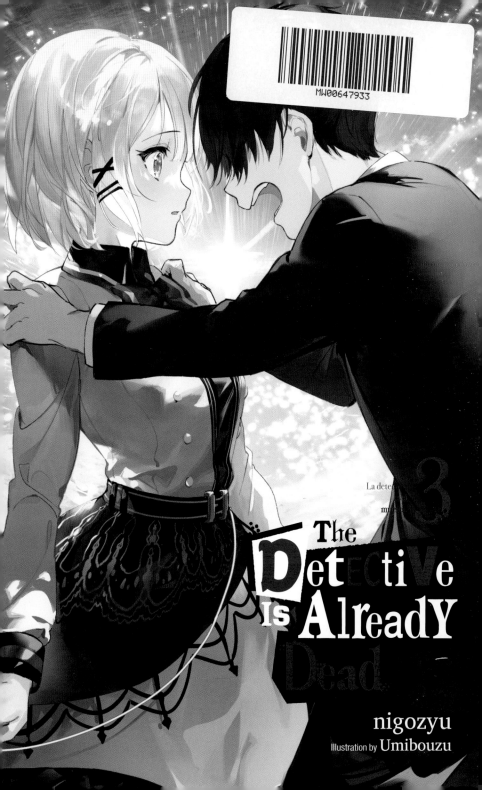

La déte...
m...

3

The
Detective
Is Already
Dead

nigozyu

Illustration by Umibouzu

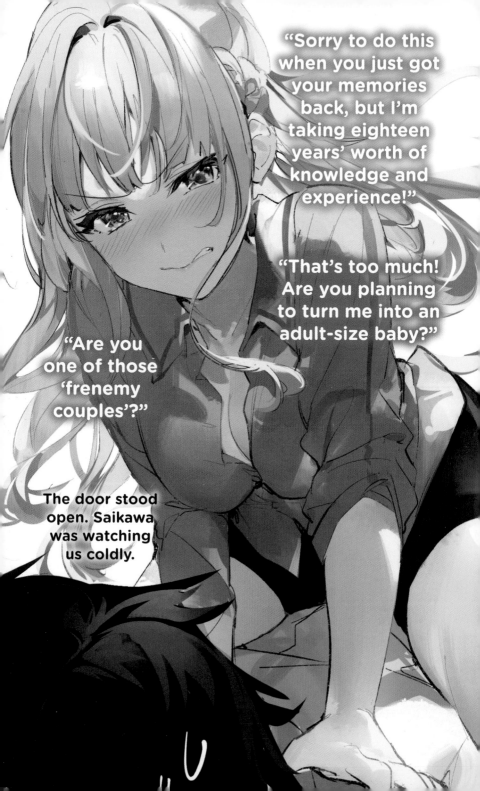

"It's Natsunagi's story, and Charlie's, and yours, Kimizuka. It belongs to each of you. So all that matters is the question of what you want to do. I think that's enough."

Siesta

Occupation	**Maid**
Age	**Unknown**
Best Dish	**Apple pie**
Favorite Music	**Classical**
Favorite Movie Genre	**Gangster films**
Special Skill	**Instant memorization**
Interests	**Napping, teasing Kimihiko**
Code	**"Do whatever it takes for your employer, even betraying them."**

Pale-silver hair,

blue eyes,

features as even and beautiful

as a sculpture. And she was wearing…

a maid uniform?

Aside from the outfit,

the girl was identical

to the former ace detective,

and her identity was——

"As long as you had Siesta, you didn't need anything else, did you?"

"Don't worry about it."

I spoke carelessly, hoping to keep Natsunagi from saying what she was about to say next.

"Before I met her, I was alone anyway."

A thousand nights, alone together

The Detective Is Already Dead

3

nigozyu

Illustration by **Umibouzu**

New York

The Detective Is Already Dead, Vol. 3

nigozyu

Translation by Taylor Engel
Cover art by Umibouzu

TANTEI HA MO, SHINDEIRU. Vol.3
©nigozyu 2020
First published in Japan in 2020 by KADOKAWA CORPORATION, Tokyo.
English translation rights arranged with KADOKAWA CORPORATION, Tokyo, through TUTTLE-MORI AGENCY, INC., Tokyo.

English translation © 2022 by Yen Press, LLC

Yen On
150 West 30th Street, 19th Floor
New York, NY 10001

Visit us at yenpress.com
facebook.com/yenpress
twitter.com/yenpress
yenpress.tumblr.com
instagram.com/yenpress

First Yen On Edition: March 2022

Yen On is an imprint of Yen Press, LLC.
The Yen On name and logo are trademarks of Yen Press, LLC.

Library of Congress Cataloging-in-Publication Data
Names: nigozyu, author. | Umibouzu, illustrator. | Engel, Taylor, translator.
Title: The detective is already dead / nigozyu ; illustration by Umibouzu ;
    translation by Taylor Engel.
Other titles: Tantei wa Mou, Shindeiru. English
Description: First Yen On edition. | New York, NY : Yen On, 2021.
Identifiers: LCCN 2021012132 | ISBN 9781975325756 (v. 1 ; trade paperback);
    ISBN 9781975325770 (v. 2 ; trade paperback)
    ISBN 9781975325794 (v. 3 ; trade paperback)
Subjects: GSAFD: Mystery fiction.
Classification: LCC PL873.5.I46 T3613 2021 | DDC 895.63/6—dc23
LC record available at https://lccn.loc.gov/2021012132

ISBNs: 978-1-9753-2579-4 (paperback)
       978-1-9753-2580-0 (ebook)

10 9 8 7 6 5 4 3 2 1

WOR

Printed in the United States of America

The Detective Is Already Dead

3

Contents

6 years ago, Nagisa

I was on the shore, listening to the ripples.

Plish, plash—little waves surged in, then retreated. My anxiety and pain faded, and my heart grew quiet. Listening to the ocean's voice here at the waterline was the only thing I looked forward to.

"What are you doing over there?"

Out of nowhere, I heard an unfamiliar voice behind me. It was a girl's voice—cool and clear, but certainly not cold.

"...Listening to the ocean," I answered, although I'd tensed up a little; I hadn't expected to run into anyone else here.

"Just listening? You're not looking at it?"

"Well, I mean, you can't see it now."

You really couldn't; it was nighttime. During the day, the sea shone like emeralds, but the only light at this hour came from the stars, and the water was black. That's why I was just enjoying the murmur of the waves.

"Couldn't you come during the day, then?"

I felt the girl sit down beside me. She'd struck me as kind of mature at first, but from the location of her voice, she seemed to be my height. Were we about the same age?

"I'd like to. They'd notice if I did, though." I kept the conversation going, opening up to her a bit.

"They'd notice? Who's 'they'?"

"...The thing is, I'm sick. I really should be in my hospital room. The bed is hard, and just lying there all the time hurts, so sometimes I sneak out here."

These moments were my only comfort, when I could escape for a little while from the painful treatments and endless boredom.

"Never mind that. Who are you? I don't think I recognize your voice."
It was nice to get to talk with a girl my age, so I asked her a question of my own.

"They brought me *here* recently. There was a bit of a situation."

"...I see." When she said "here," she didn't mean the hospital. This place was an orphanage on a certain isolated island. "It's okay, though. The people who live here are all kids like us."

Kids who were as unlucky as we were. What part of that was "okay"? I knew the answer was "nothing," really; I just couldn't think of anything better to say.

"What's your name?" the girl asked.

"Number 602. That's what the adults call me," I told her.

It wasn't just me. All the children here were treated that way... But I was sure this girl would get used to it before too long. Someday she'd also be—

"Nagisa."

At first, I thought she was talking about the seashore, but no, she meant it as a name.

"You like the ocean, so that's what I'll call you," she said with a quiet smile. Or at least it seemed as if she'd smiled.

...And so I echoed her question, sending it back to her. "What's your name?"

"I don't have one. But..."

"'But'?"

"I do have a code name, I think."

Then she told me what it was, and I thought I'd never forget it as long as I lived.

I didn't want to forget.

Chapter 1

◆ To see you one more time

"The name of the one who'll wake you up someday is—Nagisa. Nagisa Natsunagi."

That was the last thing Siesta said, and then the screen went dark.

After the film ended, none of us—me, Natsunagi, Saikawa, or Charlie—could speak right away. Silent moments ticked past, and my mind buzzed with the memories of what I'd just seen, the three years I'd spent traveling with Siesta.

We'd met on a hijacked airplane at ten thousand meters. Then, after an incident at my middle school, I'd set off on a journey with her. Our lives had been one long, dazzling adventure—and finally, our fight with the secret organization SPES had brought us to London, where we'd met a mysterious orphan named Alicia. She'd joined us as a proxy detective. However, Alicia had another personality, although she didn't know it herself. That shadow personality's name was Hel, and she was taking innocent lives on the streets of London.

To save Alicia, we headed for the enemy's hideout in pursuit of Hel. There we encountered the enemy leader, who told us what the group really was. Then Siesta plunged into her final battle with Hel.

Yes, I'd finally remembered everything.

What had happened on that island a year ago.

Why the detective was already dead.

The one who'd taken Siesta's life that day was—

"It's me."

* * *

Natsunagi murmured into the stillness. "Siesta… I'm the one who…"

"No." I couldn't let her finish. Reflexively, I cut her off. "You didn't do anything, Natsunagi. Not personally. So…"

That was something I'd told Alicia—no, Natsunagi, when she'd used Cerberus's seed to make herself look like Alicia. It was true, though: Natsunagi hadn't done anything. Even if she'd physically committed a crime, the criminal was her other personality, Hel. Natsunagi had nothing to do with the heart-hunting incidents, or with killing Siesta. She hadn't done a—

"I'm sorry."

The lights in the room came up, and for some reason, Natsunagi turned to me and apologized. Her eyes were wet with tears.

"I'm sorry I took someone so precious away from you, Kimizuka."

Her fingers approached my face. I thought she might shove them into my mouth, the way she'd done that one time, but instead her slim fingertips wiped my eyes.

"…Sorry."

I was the one who'd been crying.

I thought I'd gotten over most of this stuff, but apparently not. I had to admit it: I still hadn't managed to shake my lingering attachment to Siesta.

"So my memories were artificial," Natsunagi said softly, looking down. "Even my 'heart transplant': I only stole Siesta's heart. I bet those child-hood memories of always being in the hospital were residual memories of my time as SPES's prisoner. —As a person, I was always empty."

Natsunagi had said those things frequently: She was a fake. She couldn't become anyone. She couldn't escape her small birdcage and fly away.

I'd heard Alicia put herself down that way, too. She'd talked about her amnesia like a dark room without light or sound.

Now that I'd retrieved that year-old memory, when I looked at Natsunagi, her image and Alicia's blurred together. The Alicia I'd met in London last year had gone on to become Nagisa Natsunagi.

"Nagisa, come here and sit for a little while."

Natsunagi's shoulders were trembling. Saikawa called to her softly, and they sat down on the concrete floor together. As the older one, letting her do the comforting wasn't my finest moment, but right now, I was grateful.

"You mean your memories were tampered with?" Charlie spoke up next. "Nagisa's...and yours, Kimizuka." She glanced at me. "In Nagisa's case, we should probably assume they did it to soften the shock to her mind."

I suspected Fuubi Kase, the redheaded detective, had been the one responsible. She must have done it on Siesta's orders, to save Natsunagi.

"And I *forgot*."

The fact that I'd met Natsunagi before.

The reason Siesta was dead.

What "SPES" actually meant, and the identity of Seed, their leader.

That pollen had taken my memories of those few hours on that island.

"But you remembered, didn't you, Charlie?"

Charlie and I had come face-to-face with Seed last year at the enemy's hideout. He'd introduced himself as the parent of all pseudohumans and told us what SPES's real objective was. He'd claimed to be a literal seed who'd flown to this planet from outer space; he'd said his survival instincts were driving him to subjugate humanity. Then I'd gone to Siesta, but Charlie had stayed back at the lab and kept the enemy pinned down. That meant she hadn't gotten hit with the pollen, which meant she'd kept her memories.

"Yes. I had no idea you didn't remember, Kimizuka. After all, we weren't comparing notes on every little thing... Especially since it's, you know, us." Charlie laughed at herself a little.

When Charlie and I met on that cruise, we hadn't seen each other in a year. Then, on the deck of that luxury liner, we'd faced off against Chameleon, our sworn enemy. He'd told us he'd killed Siesta, but he was mistaken. Bet he'd never even suspected that Siesta had stopped her own heart.

"Charlie, I—" Natsunagi stood up suddenly, but...

"Don't say anything." Charlie didn't even look at her. "I know it isn't your fault. Really, I do. I just...haven't completely come to terms yet. Wait a little while."

"...Okay."

That made sense; Charlie had only just learned how Siesta had really died. The girl standing next to her had had a hand in the death of the teacher she loved and respected. There was no simple platitude she could offer.

Just what sort of *decision* were we supposed to make in a situation like this? Once again, heavy silence filled the unfamiliar room.

"First of all..." After a brief pause, a girl's clear, carrying voice spoke. "It's all right, calm down. Your hands squeeze. Your shoulders roll. Your breathing is rhythmic. Close your eyes, take a deep breath, then exhale. Your blood circulates. When you open your eyes, your cloudy vision will be clear."

The voice was Saikawa's, and I'd heard her say those words before. It was her charm for relieving tension. "Once you've finished that, why don't we have some tea?" The smile she gave us was as appealing as you'd expect an idol singer's smile to be.

"Geez. Seriously, why are you the most mature one here?"

"Heh-heh! Because I'm far more *experienced* than you are, Kimizuka... Experienced."

"Don't try to suggest something with that. You're an idol, Saikawa. Remember?"

I swear, this middle schooler... Well, that had probably been better than letting the mood stay heavy. With that thought, I turned to leave—and then, with a jolt, I remembered we were here because we'd been kidnapped.

"So where's the kidnapper?"

I had a bad feeling about this, and I looked back.

"*A tea party*, hm? That sounds nice. Do let me join you."

The next instant, I sensed someone besides the four of us.

"Who's there?!"

On reflex, I reached for the figure...but the next thing I knew, I was flying through the air. I saw the ceiling, and then— "Ow!"

My back crashed into the ground. Something like an electric shock raced through me, and my eyes squeezed shut.

"Next time you attempt to touch this body, I'll crush every bone in yours."

Not fair. I slowly opened my eyes, planning to hit the culprit who'd thrown me with a few well-chosen words—then froze.

"You're..."

The person in front of me was extremely familiar.

She had pale silver hair. Features as beautiful as a sculpture. And she was wearing...a maid uniform? Her taste in clothing wasn't quite what I remembered, but her appearance was definitely right. For three years, I'd spent every moment with this girl, whose name was—

"—Siesta."

There was no mistake. My former partner was standing right there.

◆ Because you said to wear a maid uniform

"Please, go on. Order anything you like," said the white-haired girl in the maid uniform. We were all seated around a table.

The five of us had relocated to a café for our tea party. It was roomy, but I didn't see any other guests. Apparently, she'd reserved the whole place.

The person who'd brought us here said, "There's no need to hold back on my account. Kimihiko's paying." She was elegantly sipping tea, a step ahead of the rest of us.

"Well, you're welcome to hold back on *my* account, Siesta," I retorted at the girl who was sitting in *the guest of honor's seat.*

With that dazzling white hair and those blue eyes, she was undeniably my former partner. But...

"You really do look just like Ma'am," Charlie murmured as she watched Siesta drink her tea, then nod approvingly.

This Siesta *wasn't the real thing.*

Of course she wasn't. The detective had been dead for a year.

"Charlotte. As I told you, I'm merely *a robot.*"

She'd explained as much on our way here.

This Siesta was *a living android who had been created based on Siesta's body, memories, and abilities.*

"...You're sure you're not Siesta?" I asked. She looked completely human to me.

"Yes. Unlike Mistress Siesta, I don't call you Kimi."

"I see. Well, you're right, the real one wouldn't have pulled a shoulder-throw on me. She would have let me rest my head on her lap instead."

"...I've run a database inquiry, and that never actually happened."

"Hey, if you're going to turn away, be more subtle about it. If you're based on Siesta, you should be fonder of me."

"I am contemptuous of you precisely because I am based on Mistress Siesta."

"Okay, I want all my tears back."

This was weird. The somber mood was vanishing like it never existed.

"What, did you rehearse this? You sound like an elderly married couple."

"Yui, don't compare them to a married couple. At least make it a veteran comedy duo."

Saikawa and Charlie were sitting across from me. For some reason, they were both glaring at me. *Gimme a break, this isn't my fault. It's all the detective's fault... But this isn't the time to be saying things like that.*

"Since you kidnapped us, I assume you have some sort of business with us? Or did Siesta tell you to do this before she died?"

Siesta was the one who'd kidnapped us and shown us that record of the past. The room where she'd locked us up was part of the hideout where she lived.

"Yes, Mistress Siesta made various preparations before that day arrived. Finding you was one of them; placing me here as backup was another. She instructed me to tell you the truth."

"Would that normally take a kidnapping, though?"

"I had to. I couldn't have told you otherwise."

Then Siesta turned her eyes to the one person who'd been silent all this time.

"Nagisa."

That name was the last thing the detective had left behind.

Next to me, Nagisa looked up and heard the ace detective's last words.

"Let me say this in Mistress Siesta's stead: Thank you."

The mood had been hazy all this time, but those words were like a wind that changed it once again. It felt as if SIESTA had appeared just to say this.

The rest of us took those words to heart right along with Natsunagi.

"Thanks to you, Mistress Siesta's will has not vanished. In addition, preserving your life and sending you to school was her final wish—and her job. Consequently, you have my gratitude. Thank you." SIESTA quietly bowed her head.

Natsunagi faltered. "I'm…" Her gaze swam and her lips formed soundless syllables.

We could say the "right" things all day, but there was no guarantee that they'd ease Natsunagi's mind. Responsibility for the past seemed to weigh on her, and she looked down. Silence descended again.

"Why don't we have our tea while we talk? This place has excellent apple pie," SIESTA said quietly, and I realized that pie and black tea had appeared on our table.

"…That takes me back," Natsunagi murmured, putting a small piece of pie crust in her mouth.

I noticed she was noting the memories, not the flavor.

"…Anyway, SIESTA." I was speaking for all of us as I asked about the things we needed to know. "Why did you choose now to get us together and tell us about the past? Why hide the truth for so long?"

One year. That was how long it had been since Siesta died. If SIESTA's mission had been to tell us the truth, why hadn't she made contact sooner?

"There are several reasons." SIESTA began to explain, holding up fingers as she did so. "First, it took Mistress Siesta a long time to suppress Hel's vicious personality, which lies dormant in that body, and stabilize Nagisa."

That was something Siesta had said during our last conversation—she'd mentioned that it might take a long time to seal Hel. Natsunagi herself had told me that she'd only recently been well enough to attend school. So it had taken a year to get all of that in place, huh?

"Second, I was waiting for the four of you to be on the same page emotionally."

"Us?"

"Yes, because that was Mistress Siesta's last wish."

Right. That was the message from Siesta that Natsunagi had given me: Natsunagi, Saikawa, Charlie, and I were her legacy.

"But," Charlie broke in, "why 'the four of us'? Especially Kimizuka... Do we need him?"

"Hey, Charlie. Why are you acting like that's a natural question to have?"

"It does seem as though she was torn about whether or not to include Kimihiko Kimizuka until the very end."

"Why? I should be first! I was her assistant, remember?"

"Kimizuka, you're not going to tell us the events of those three years were all a lie, are you? Are we about to learn you were just her stalker the whole time?" Saikawa asked.

"Saikawa, you have the best eyes here. What exactly did you see in those memories?"

It was hopeless. The second the mood eases a bit, these people launch into comedy routines.

"But..." As if she'd read my mind, Natsunagi gave Siesta an earnest look. "You probably haven't told us the most important reason yet, have you."

Why had Siesta assembled the four of us now? Why had she told us the truth? That's what Natsunagi was asking.

Siesta's eyes narrowed, and she mentioned someone I'd forgotten about until just now.

It was the leader of SPES and, most likely, our greatest enemy.

"Over the past year, Seed hasn't done anything of note. Recently, though, the situation seems to be changing."

She was right. Saikawa's sapphire incident and Chameleon's attack on the ship were probably cases in point. What had he been trying to do during that year?

"Stopping him is your job, Nagisa." Siesta set her cup back in its saucer.

"My job..." The heavy role she'd been handed made Natsunagi lower her eyes. Usually, she would have thumped her chest, bursting with confidence, and accepted. However, now that she'd found out what was in her past...

"It's not like she has to do this alone." I gulped down the rest of my tea without coming up for air, then turned to Siesta. "Saikawa, Charlie, and I all agree that we have to take down SPES. Natsunagi shouldn't have to feel any more responsible for it."

Natsunagi might have voluntarily inherited the ace detective's will, but Saikawa, Charlie, and I were also part of Siesta's legacy. Defeating SPES was a goal we all had in common.

"Yes, that's true. However, Nagisa's role in this doesn't compare to yours, Yui's, or Charlotte's. After all..." Siesta drew a little breath. "Nagisa is *the ace detective*." As she spoke, she was clearly emphasizing the term.

"What about it? If you mean it's a little different from being a regular detective, Natsunagi gets that already."

Siesta had also called herself the ace detective, but she'd had very little in common with the normal concept of *detective*. Generally in a mystery, you're not going to run into a detective who fights pseudohumans and aliens. Considering everything that had happened so far, Natsunagi had to be well aware of that already.

"...I see. So Mistress Siesta didn't even tell you that." Siesta gave a pensive little nod. "The ace detective isn't what you think it is, Kimihiko." She spoke as if she'd read my mind. "You're correct that it isn't someone who merely solves crimes in the ordinary way. However, when we use the term 'the ace detective,' it generally means something different—"

"Wait."

Just then, the table jolted noisily and Charlie stood up, spilling our tea. "If you say any more, you'll be in violation of the *Federal Charter*." She leveled an accusing glare at Siesta. I had no idea what this Federal Charter was.

"It doesn't matter. They're already involved." Siesta looked around the table at us, then went on, her face still expressionless.

"The ace detective is a position. It's one of the twelve shields that protect the world—the Tuners."

◆ The enemies of the world and the twelve shields

"The Tuners... So that's what this is about..."

"Huh? You knew about this, too, Kimizuka?" Saikawa asked; she'd noticed my grave expression. "What on earth are the Tuners?"

"No idea."

"Don't act as if you know anything ever again." The young idol was suddenly very cold.

"This world is under near constant threat."

Ignoring the witty repartee Saikawa and I had going, SIESTA went on with her explanation.

"These crises strike regularly, and sometimes several happen at once. In an effort to combat them, an international organization has secretly appointed individuals known as 'Tuners.'"

Someone created to face the world's crises... Now that she mentioned it, I got the feeling Siesta had said something like that once. Something about how she existed to protect the world. About having that sort of DNA.

"There are twelve Tuners scattered across the globe. They are assigned various missions to handle global crises, and each occupies a different position." As she counted, she folded her fingers down, one by one. "Phantom Thief, for example. Oracle. Assassin. I'm told there's even a Magician and a Vampire."

"'Vampire'...?" *What kind of job is that? I can't imagine what sort of work they'd do.*

"Since they serve as a bulwark against threats to the world, many historical perils have been averted." SIESTA went on, explaining clearly. "Nuclear war, climate change, pandemics, impact events. In some cases, humanity itself has been the source of the threat. In others, as with SPES, threats have come to this world from elsewhere. Either way, the Tuners have always fought these crises from the shadows."

"Then without them, the world would have been destroyed and we just never knew?"

"That's right. It's even said that one of the twelve held back *the King of*

Terror who should have attacked in 1999." SIESTA listed a major prophecy by Nostradamus that had once rocked the world to its foundations, as if it was just one possibility among many. "The world line on which we're living now may actually be a future that was rewritten by the Tuners."

"Don't tell me... Are you saying it's actually possible to change history?"

"Declaring that what can't be observed doesn't exist is the height of arrogance. Besides, you know of *one such case* personally, don't you, Kimihiko?"

I searched my memory for something applicable and came up with...

"—The sacred text."

It was the book Hel had told me about a year ago, *the one that held a record of the future.* Could its author have been someone who actually knew the future?

...No, I couldn't afford to take things that far off topic right now. More importantly, now that I knew about the Tuners, I could put together one thing from what SIESTA had said so far with near certainty.

"So Siesta was a Tuner, then."

SIESTA affirmed my guess wordlessly, by taking a sip of tea.

Siesta had been one of the twelve Tuners who saved the world—and her position had been ace detective. Her mission had been to bring SPES to heel.

She'd never said a word about it. However ...

"......"

Charlie was biting her lip, and one look at her profile told me it was true. Siesta had talked about fighting the enemies of the world almost as if it was a mission she'd been given, but there had been something much larger behind it.

"That said..." While I was still thinking, SIESTA went on. "Last year, when Mistress Siesta died, the seat of ace detective became vacant. Since then, no one has been in charge of subjugating SPES."

"What are the other Tuners doing? They could take over for her."

"It's not like SPES is the only global crisis," Charlie said. "The other eleven Tuners have jobs of their own to do."

"I see. So SPES isn't the world's only enemy..."

Then even as we spoke, some other threat was heading for the planet… and someone else was fighting it?

"Returning to the subject at hand…," SIESTA said, looking at Natsunagi. "If nothing changes, it's likely that you will be named as the next ace detective."

"…! I…will?"

Natsunagi hadn't been expecting that, and her eyes widened.

"Nothing's settled yet, of course. However, you do have the former ace detective's heart, and you've taken up her will. You can also take full advantage of powers ordinary humans don't have. Many will feel you have what it takes to fill the position."

I see. So Natsunagi hadn't just inherited Siesta's heart and her will. They thought she had the capacity to make the most of her power as well. But…

"Siesta won't speak through Natsunagi anymore."

During that battle with Chameleon on the ship, Siesta had borrowed Natsunagi's body to appear to me—and then she'd vanished. It hadn't been a miracle or a deus ex machina development. She'd loved teasing me, and she'd shown me a transient daydream.

"Yes, I'm aware of that. And so"—SIESTA turned back to Natsunagi— "in Mistress Siesta's place, let me ask you, one more time: Nagisa, do you really intend to inherit the ace detective's will?" She was testing Natsunagi's resolve.

"I…" Natsunagi's voice was trembling.

"What if…," I cut in. I didn't have a plan or anything. It just seemed too mean to ask Natsunagi to make a decision like this right now. "Let's say that, someday, Natsunagi takes over as ace detective. What would she have to do first?"

It didn't have to be right now. I was simply asking about a hypothetical future.

"Let's see…," SIESTA said. She sipped what was left of the tea in her cup, and her eyes scanned the four of us.

"In that case, I would like you to *find the mistake* that was hidden in the past I showed you."

◆ Occupation: student, occasional assistant

The day after that, I was at school, sitting in class.

I'd completely forgotten that summer break classes were a thing.

This may seem like it's coming out of nowhere, but I'm a regular student before I'm a detective's assistant, at least as far as society is concerned. The other day, I'd sauntered off on a cruise and gotten kidnapped et cetera on what was supposed to be my break, but...apparently students in their last year of high school don't even truly get respite during summer vacation.

"It's still only been fifteen minutes?" A glance at the clock on the wall plunged me into despair. This class had begun in the morning as a "summer extracurricular," and it had been dragging so slowly that I suspected it might last forever. There was still more than half an hour left before lunch.

"Guess I'll just sleep."

Sleeping is a student's duty. I've heard that sleeping children grow well. Perfect, I was just thinking I'd like to be three centimeters taller. Come to think of it, Siesta slept a lot too. Is that why she grew so well in all those intriguing places?

"...Huh?"

Yikes, was that a shitty thing to think?

I was tired. That had to be it. After all, way too much had happened yesterday.

My seat was at the very back of the room, on the hall side. I slumped over my desk, shut my eyes, and got the inside of my head in order.

Yesterday, Siesta had told us that the world was protected by twelve Tuners, and that Natsunagi was about to be appointed to one of those positions: ace detective.

If Natsunagi took that role, the first thing Siesta said she'd have to do was *find the mistake*. Then she'd filled us in on the details. According to her, there had been a certain *error* in the footage we'd been shown from last year. If Natsunagi wasn't sure whether to become the ace detective, she could work on finding that mistake first, and decide later. That was the last thing she'd said before she released us.

In other words, what I—or Natsunagi—needed to do now was find some sort of error hidden in the revelations about last year.

"We don't have any clues, though," I muttered, quietly enough that nobody would hear.

...The next thing I knew, the room had gotten kind of noisy. Class had ended while I wasn't paying attention, and it was finally lunch. I just had to get through two more periods in the afternoon, and then today's extracurriculars would be over. Figuring I'd go grab a convenience store bento the way I always did, I raised my head, and that's when it happened.

"Oh."

I made eye contact with a girl in the corridor—Nagisa Natsunagi. She was probably headed to the cafeteria with some friends; she was with three or four other girls who all looked sort of trendy.

Perfect timing. We needed to discuss our plan of action. I stood up, meaning to set up a time to meet after school, but—

"......"

She averted her eyes, avoiding me.

Her friends giggled, whispering something to her. Natsunagi waved her hands and shook her head in emphatic denial, and they all walked off.

Is this hell? Felt like every eye in the classroom was on me. I dropped into my chair again and went back to sleep.

"How long are you planning to nap?!"

After class, a joking voice woke me up.

My eyes were blurry with sleep. I rubbed them, and a hazy figure came into focus. "Hey, I just resolved two incidents. I was finally settling down."

I hadn't been sleeping *all* that time. True to my status as a trouble magnet, I'd just finished clearing up some minor issues my classmates had brought to me after school.

"And actually, I'm not talking to you anymore, Natsunagi." I glared at her, remembering the way she'd treated me earlier.

She was sitting sideways at the desk in front of mine, turned to face me.

"Look, I'm sorry. Geez, you've got bedhead." Natsunagi marched right into my personal space, combing my hair with her fingers.

"What are you, Siesta?"

"Only half." In the dim orange light that lanced through the windows, she gave a faint smile.

The sun was almost down, and the two of us were the only ones left in the classroom.

"And? What do you want, Natsunagi?" I smacked her hand away from my head.

"What do you mean, 'what'? You sent me a signal at lunch, remember?"

"And who was it that ignored it and went off somewhere?"

Nothing hurts worse than knowing the girls at your school are whispering about you, all right?

"...Well, they teased me." Natsunagi gave me a reproachful look. "They were, you know, asking if you and I were 'together like *that*.'"

"Don't get embarrassed about that kind of gossip."

"I didn't mean it that way." Natsunagi puffed out her cheeks and tugged on my bangs, as if she was trying to communicate something. Seriously, what?

"Listen, you sleep too much. Just how many hours do you think I waited?"

"Bold words from somebody with red marks on her face."

"Hey, why didn't you tell me sooner?!"

"And you should wipe off your drool."

"I'll double-kill you!"

Natsunagi pushed my head down onto my desk. Not fair...

"...So? What did you need?" she asked again, after she'd finished wiping her face. Her eyes were on the setting sun outside the window. It was almost down.

"...Right."

I started to bring up what I'd been planning to talk about... But, for some reason, the words wouldn't come.

It wasn't just me. Natsunagi had to know what I wanted to talk about. When it came down to it, though, neither of us could broach that subject.

"So you've got friends, huh?" I made random small talk instead.

"What a sad thing to say..." Natsunagi gave me a pitying look. "How do you always spend your lunch breaks?"

"I've got an extra special place, so it's fine." Although thanks to a certain somebody, I'd ended up accidentally sleeping through lunch today.

"A place where you're likely to eat lunch alone all the time, Kimizuka? ...Like the bathroom?"

"Do you get that you're being seriously insulting right now?"

I knew she inherited the detective's last will, but she didn't have to inherit the part where she constantly makes fun of me, too. With a sigh, I got up. "In that case, come on, I'll show it to you right now."

Natsunagi's mouth dropped open.

"Huh? You're taking me to the bathroom? I, um, I don't think that's really..."

"I never said that, and I definitely don't need you getting bashful about it."

◆ A thousand nights, alone together

"This way."

Walking ahead of Natsunagi, I stepped over the Do Not Enter barrier and climbed a short flight of stairs. There was a padlocked metal door at the top.

"Kimizuka, do you have the key?"

"No. But there's no lock I can't open."

"Ooh, aren't you cool."

"I've been kidnapped and locked up so much that I picked up the skill naturally."

"I stand corrected. You aren't cool at all."

"There, got it."

After a few seconds of twisting a special wire around, the lock clicked and came right off. I pushed the door open and stepped through—into the wind.

"Wow..." Natsunagi sounded impressed as she followed me out.

This was my extra special place: the roof. The sun had set, and stars twinkled in the dark, cloudless sky.

"What do you think? Even by yourself, this isn't bad. Lunch tastes extra good when you eat it on the roof." I sat down with my back against the tall fence.

"You don't need to be alone, though, do you?" Natsunagi sat down beside me. She sounded a little exasperated. "Why don't you make some friends?"

"It's not that I don't make friends. More that I can't."

"Congratulations, you found the worst sentence to say aloud."

That was a sucky award to have on my record.

"Well, you could count me, you know. On your 'friends' counter." Natsunagi stretched her legs straight out, fiddling with the hem of her short skirt. "I mean, we don't have to be friends, specifically. There are, you know, all sorts of other relationships…"

"Like 'underling'?"

"Let me ask again, just because. Exactly what were you to Siesta, Kimizuka?"

The conversation wasn't going in the direction I wanted it to.

Meanwhile, Natsunagi's shoulders slumped. "Well, I mean…it's pretty nice to have a friend you can talk to about anything. Plus, I'm cute." She poked her index fingers into her own cheeks, mugging self-consciously.

"I've never had a friend, so I wouldn't know."

"You're messed up, you know that?" Natsunagi pouted, looking kind of appalled. "It's amazing you managed to get along with Siesta when you're like this."

"…I don't remember getting along all that well." I thought back over those hectic years. "We fought once every three days."

"And then you'd apologize first?"

"Most of the time, yeah. But sometimes I hung in there and ignored her for a week or so."

"And then?"

"She started to get incredibly fidgety and restless."

"Geez, how cute is Siesta!"

"Then, when I finally spoke to her, for a second she'd get all relieved, and then…"

"She'd go back to looking cranky and say, 'Are you stupid, Kimi?'"

"Hey, got it in one. Way to go; you could get a Level 1 certification in Siesta Studies."

We cracked up a little.

"Still, we fought so much that one time we made up this rule."

"So you wouldn't fight?"

"Yeah. The day after we fought, we had to go to an amusement park together."

"Wh-what's the point...?"

"You know: Going to an amusement park together when your relationship's awkward is pretty hellish."

"Ohhh, and since you didn't want that, you figured you'd learn to get by without fighting... And? Did it work?"

"Yeah. Thanks to that, we got into the habit of riding the teacups once every three days."

"Thanks for that nonsensical joke. Extremely funny." Natsunagi raised both hands in an exaggerated shrug of boredom, palms up. These American-style jokes are fun. "And actually..." This time, she seemed to be testing me somehow. "You always seem to enjoy talking about Siesta, Kimizuka."

That remark sounded rather pointed.

"...Nah. I don't want to talk about her. At this point, I have absolutely no interest in her."

"Uh, seriously, it's way too late for anyone to believe that now." Natsunagi waved a hand dismissively, straight-faced. *She's got to be kidding. That can't be right.*

"Still."

Natsunagi looked away.

"As long as you had Siesta, you didn't need anything else, did you?"

She finally brought up the subject we'd both been unconsciously avoiding. Her profile looked a little lonely.

"Don't worry about it." I spoke carelessly, hoping to keep Natsunagi from saying what she was about to say next. "Before I met her, I was alone anyway."

That meant it wasn't Natsunagi's fault. Nobody thought she'd taken everything. More importantly, I wouldn't let anybody say a thing like that.

"You're nice, Kimizuka." Natsunagi's voice sounded muffled. Before I knew it, she'd buried her face in her knees. "It's no good, though. Even when I'm talking to my friends, or you're trying to encourage me, I just can't get that sight out of my head. Of me, taking Siesta's heart—"

She broke off.

The roof was deserted except for us. The only sound was the whisper of the night wind.

Natsunagi's hands had taken Siesta's life.

That was an incontrovertible fact. Even if it had been her other personality that had done it… Even if it had been what Siesta herself had wanted, that wouldn't ease her feelings of guilt. That was what she thought, at least.

"Besides, it wasn't just Siesta. Those other people in London were completely innocent, and I—"

That was another heavy curse that would bind her guilt to her permanently. No matter who tried to encourage her or what they said, she would never forgive herself.

Under the circumstances, there was only one thing I could do.

"Grumpy gills."

I ran my index finger down Natsunagi's sailor-suited back.

"Yeek!" Natsunagi gave a cute little shriek that I had never heard from her before, then hastily clapped a hand over her mouth. "Wha, what, wha-wha-wha-wha-wha-wha-wha-wha-wha-wha-wha-wha!" Her face went so red I could tell even in the darkness. She glared at me, her lips trembling.

"Haaah. Listen, Natsunagi."

"I'm not done being mad yet!"

"Huh? Wasn't this one of your fetishes?"

"D-d-d-d-d-d-d-d-d-d-double-kill!"

"There we go. That sounds like you."

"Don't use people's catchphrases to gauge how they're feeling!" Natsunagi pummeled my side. She really was feeling better.

"A long time ago..." As I spoke, I was thinking about those memories from last year. "Ages back, when I lost all hope and just curled up in a corner...Siesta encouraged me."

"You mean..." Natsunagi stopped hitting me.

Yeah, you know about it too. It was back when Chameleon had taken Alicia—in other words, Natsunagi—to SPES's hideout. I'd completely given up, but Siesta had thumped me on the back and shown me what I needed to do again.

"So I'll thump you on the back or hold your hand whenever you need it, too."

"...Except what you did was run a finger down my back."

...Well, it's basically the same thing. Pretty much.

"For now, you can be discouraged as long as you want." I moved away from the fence, then lay down on my back, right there on the roof. All I could see was the starry sky. "You can order a bunch of takeout and stress eat, or watch sad movies and cry all your tears out at once. You can curse how unfair the world always is and scream a string of obscenities, or if you're the type who blows off stress with karaoke, I'll keep you company till the sun comes up. If none of that is enough to make you stop feeling guilty, then at least let me take half of it. It's not like you're the only one to blame here. I couldn't save Siesta either. So at least...let me carry some of that pain for you."

"Kimizuka..."

Natsunagi looked down at me, almost dazed.

...Hm. Had I made myself look too cool? In that case...

"Well, you know. If I say this, it feels like I'm going to kinda screw myself here, but..." I hesitated, then finally made up my mind and told her. "I'm used to being abused by girls."

That meant carrying Natsunagi's pain for her was nothing.

"...Pfft!"

She burst out laughing.

"Ha-ha! Aaah-ha-ha-ha-ha-ha-ha-ha!"

"—It wasn't *that* funny!"

"Seriously, what?! Why did you start confessing your fetishes all of a sudden?"

"...! Look, I was trying! To cheer you up! All right?!"

Rgh, why did it turn out like this? Not fair...

"So you cheered me up by confessing that you're a masochist... Wow, that's not good. You're in even worse shape than I thought, Kimizuka."

"Wha...! Quit! No more laughing! And you're no different!"

"Noooo, I don't think that word means quite the same thing for you as it does for me."

"—! Haaah, I shouldn't have said it... No, okay, that was a lie. I was just going for a laugh, to cheer you up; that's not actually a thing for me..." I sat up, stumbling through a denial, but then—

"I swear, that's so stupid."

With a thump, Natsunagi buried her face in my chest.

"Really, really stupid."

She laughed as she said it...and the next thing I knew, she was crying.

She bit her lip, careful not to let any sobs escape, but my shirt was damp with tears.

"Which of us is?"

I knew even as I said it, though.

Whether she was mad, or happy, or laughing, or crying, she always did it with all her might. That was Nagisa Natsunagi's true essence. Her passion.

"You toughed it out really well." Gazing at the distant stars, I stroked her head.

Natsunagi had the red ribbon Siesta had left to her in her hair.

"...—, ...—!"

On the roof that night, a torrent of passionate rain fell.

Even so, the stars were infuriatingly pretty.

◆ I swear to God, I didn't...

After that, we went back inside and walked through the shadowy building, lighting our way with our smartphones.

The school was totally dark; at this hour, the trek was like some sort of test of courage.

"All right. Now that you've stopped crying, Kimizuka, we'll have to think about what to do next." Natsunagi, who was walking next to me, smacked her own cheeks sharply.

"You are such a liar. My shirt is all soggy with your tears and your snot." On the roof, Natsunagi had cried on my chest for fifteen minutes or so. My school uniform had been nobly sacrificed in the service of helping her feel better.

"Ngh... You said you'd take half of it!"

"Now that I've calmed down, that's way too embarrassing, so please quit."

"—May I have half of your life?"

"I swear on all that's good and holy that I didn't say that!" *Also, her impression sounds nothing like me. Geez. The minute she feels better, she starts in with this.*

"You gave me a ring, too, though."

"...That happened a year ago. Doesn't count."

That said, I'd held hands with Natsunagi like this when she was Alicia, too...

"...Wh-why exactly did you just take my hand like it was natural?"

Now who's on the defensive? Natsunagi sounded a little flustered. Ordinarily she's a total sadist with me, but even she's weak to surprise attacks.

"Just so you know, Natsunagi. Nobody in this world is more scared of ghosts than I am."

"Um, I don't think that's the sort of thing you can brag about."

"Besides, remember what I said on the roof? That I'd hold your hand whenever?"

"That's the most pathetic use of foreshadowing I've ever seen. And I'm getting déjà vu about this, too...," Natsunagi added quietly. Come to think of it, back when I'd only just met Siesta, we'd had a similar conversation in that haunted house at the cultural festival.

"Actually, Kimizuka, your palms are really sweaty."

"? I'm the type who stops sweating entirely when I'm scared."

"..."

"So, Natsunagi, why are *your* palms sweaty?"

"...I hate you, Kimizuka."

High school girls are hilariously cute when they dig their own graves.

"Listen... About the *finding the mistake* business SIESTA mentioned."

Natsunagi seemed to have gotten her emotions figured out a little now; she brought up that topic herself. If she was going to take over as ace detective, she'd have to find the error in those memories we'd been shown.

"Do you have any ideas, Kimizuka?"

"No, nothing. Except..."

"Except what?"

I decided to tell Natsunagi about the one thing that had been tugging at me. "She went out of her way, over a full year, to tell us what really happened back then. Why would she put a *mistake* in that?"

"...You mean this wasn't something Siesta did intentionally?"

Exactly. In life, Siesta had believed that version of the past was correct, and she had presented it to us as the truth. If there was an error in there anyway, that meant—

"Before she died, Siesta messed up."

That was the only thing I could think of. There had been another secret behind that incident last year. SIESTA was trying to get us to find it.

"But would she really have made a mistake like that? Siesta, of all people..." Natsunagi frowned skeptically.

I could understand why she'd be dubious. I'd spent three years with the ace detective, and I'd never seen her make any serious mistakes. Siesta was always right about literally everything. What could she have gotten wrong?

"So there are things even you don't know about Siesta, Kimizuka." Natsunagi tilted her head, as if it struck her as odd. "I just assumed you knew everything, right down to her bust-waist-hip measurements."

"Oh, I do know those. Of course." We'd lived together for three years. It would have been weirder if I didn't.

"...No, there's just no way. Opportunities to find those out don't come along often."

"Really? But if you touch somebody, you get a general idea of.........
Forget I said that."

Natsunagi had cautiously shaken my hand off, so I hastily corrected
myself. Just to be clear, I didn't mean "touch" so much as...you know,
"connect with" by accident. It was unavoidable. Right, that softness was
unavoidable.

Setting that aside.

"If there was some sort of mistake in those memories, wouldn't it be
faster to talk to people who were involved?" I suggested.

"Maybe so. From what Siesta was saying, we can limit ourselves to the
incident last year, right?"

"Yeah. The stuff I'd like to consign to oblivion at that cultural festival
doesn't count."

*Or rather, I don't want to dredge it up. Which is why we're going to go grill
some relevant parties in that whole chain of incidents in London and the SPES
hideout.*

"So, the people at the center of that are you, Siesta...and me. Right?"

"Yeah. On the flip side, while it would be great if there was someone
besides us that we could talk to, I dunno..."

The first person who came to mind was Charlie. She'd been with us
when we invaded SPES's hideout. She hadn't mentioned anything when
the topic of finding the mistake first came up, though, which probably
meant it hadn't rung any bells for her.

"Um, then, what about...the enemy leader?"

"Seed, huh? He does seem like he'd know all our cards as well as his, but
we don't even know where he is right now."

Still, she had a point. Our allies weren't the only ones who could help us
out here.

"But as far as other enemies go..."

Cerberus and Chameleon had both been involved in that incident, but
they were already dead. There was one more left, though. *The most important person.*

"Hel."

When I said the name, Natsunagi's eyes widened slightly. "But didn't
Siesta seal her inside me?"

"Yeah. Sealed. It's not like she's gone."

"So we're going to summon her? But Siesta shut her away, so…"

"One year," I reminded her. "Siesta—*the* Siesta—spent a year persuading her. I'm sure it'll be fine."

Besides, if this was a really bad move, Siesta would stop Natsunagi, even if it meant kicking up a fuss inside her. If she wasn't doing that, then it couldn't be a terrible idea. The problem was—

"How are we going to summon Hel?"

Last time Siesta surfaced in Natsunagi's body, she'd done it because I was in deep trouble, but…

"If we go back up to the roof and I push you off, just maybe, in the nick of time…"

"There is no nick of time. I'll be one hundred percent dead."

Don't put your fingertip to your chin and look all serious, as if you're thinking Would it work…? *Your assistant's life deserves more care, doesn't it?*

"Besides, even if I was in danger, Hel wouldn't come save me."

Then what should we do?

Natsunagi and I kept on thinking and coming up empty, and then…

"I overheard."

"…!"

Out of nowhere, someone interrupted and stepped in front of us, illuminating her face with a flashlight. "If you'd like to summon Hel, leave it to me."

There in the darkness, the pale-faced Siesta was standing there like a ghost.

"Nagisa, would you help me? Kimihiko's in a crisis."

"I have never seen anyone's legs give out that dramatically before, ever."

◆ The great evil returns

Fifteen minutes later, the three of us were in an apartment.

Specifically my apartment. I was currently living on the money I'd stashed away while working as Siesta's assistant.

"A guy's apartment…" Natsunagi was looking around the room. For some reason, she seemed fidgety. "Now that he has brought me into his home, oughtn't I make him take responsibility?"

"Natsunagi, I can hear your weirdly stilted-sounding thoughts from here." Although it did look like she'd cheered up a bit, so maybe I should call this a win. "And? Why are we at my house?" I asked SIESTA, who was walking all over my place as if there was nothing wrong with that.

"Because if we are going to make a lot of noise, this was the closest location where we could get away with it."

"My landlord hasn't said a word about noise being okay."

The way she just keeps going without listening to people is apparently something she inherited from the original Siesta… Still, right now, more importantly…

"Is the detective supposed to get help from the client?"

We were taking her up on her offer to summon Hel, but SIESTA was the one who'd made this request in the first place. Was it okay for us to just take her help like that?

"You really are stupid, aren't you, Kimihiko." SIESTA glanced at me. "I'm sure Mistress Siesta would have said she'd do anything, provided it was to protect the client's interests."

…I see. She wouldn't hesitate to borrow the client's help if it meant fulfilling their wish, huh?

"Well? Can you actually summon Hel?"

"Yes, of course," SIESTA said casually. "However, there are a few things I'll need. Let's see… First, is there a mirror in this apartment?"

"A mirror? I've got a full-length mirror, but…"

Although I didn't know what she was planning to use it for, I hauled out the one I kept in my bedroom closet.

"That's a very big full-length mirror."

"Yeah, I bought it so I'd be able to see the results of my daily strength training."

"Hm. You seem to have shut it in the closet, though."

"Anyway, what are you going to use this for?"

"You redirected the conversation without giving me the slightest opportunity to comment."

I had no idea what she was talking about. I was just thinking of picking my strength training routine back up, starting today. Seriously, cross my heart.

"We're going to summon Hel into this mirror."

What SIESTA said was completely crazy.

"Why so dubious?"

"Well, if you're going to bring up occult stuff out of nowhere…"

"I think the scale is more modest than giant robots and aliens."

"Yeah, but I'm more likely to believe in sci-fi than fantasy." *Does the occult count as fantasy?*

"Conversely, then, does that mean you believe what you see?" Siesta detached an object from her waist and held it out to us.

"A hand mirror?" Natsunagi looked at it, tilting her head.

It did look like an ordinary round hand mirror, but it was probably…

"One of Siesta's Seven Tools, hm?"

She'd had seven secret tools that she'd used to solve cases, way back when. There was the musket she always carried on her back and the shoes that let her move as though gravity didn't exist. Had SIESTA inherited those, too?

"This hand mirror can capture whatever is reflected in it, like a camera. I'll retrieve that recording now," she said, and various scenes surfaced and vanished in the mirror, one after another. SIESTA had said "camera," but it seemed to be more like a video camera. It held footage of Siesta and me during our travels. The memories we'd been shown in the kidnapper's lair must have been edited from some of this.

The images in the mirror zipped through in fast-forward, finally stopping on one particular scene.

"That's…London…"

The mirror showed Hel. Her red eyes were wide with shock. When we'd first fought her in London, Siesta had used this mirror to take advantage of the brainwashing effect in Hel's eyes. That was how we'd won.

"This is me too, isn't it?" Natsunagi murmured softly, watching the mirror.

This was Hel, Natsunagi's other form. I'd met her last year, naturally.

Natsunagi wore her hair differently now, and everything else—the military cap and uniform, the way she spoke, her general vibe—had changed. As I looked from one to the other, the only thing that seemed the same was the color of their eyes.

"I'll have to admit it, though." Natsunagi gazed at the mirror, confronting the reality of her other self. "All right, SIESTA. How can I meet this other me?"

"No, that's really not gonna—" I broke in. You can't let a tiger out of a painting, and you can't show a doppelganger in a mirror. However, with no hesitation, SIESTA said...

"An infinity mirror."

She went on. "Haven't you ever heard the urban legends about those?"

"Well, I hear a lot about how they're unlucky," I replied.

Natsunagi gave a little nod of agreement.

"There are rumors about them. They say you can use them to summon devils. That they can show you the past and the future."

"...!"

Natsunagi and I exchanged wide-eyed looks. Both those rumors reminded us of someone.

...However, that didn't change the fact that it seemed far too implausible.

"Nagisa, stand in front of the mirror, please."

SIESTA's expression didn't even flicker. She led Nagisa to a spot a few meters in front of the mirror. Then she gave her the hand mirror, creating an infinity mirror as both reflected Natsunagi's face.

"Let me finish getting everything ready." SIESTA took out a lit lantern and turned off the lights. It was late at night. The only light in the room was the orange flame, and it flickered eerily. Was this a necessary part of the ceremony too?

"Now let's move back a little. Nagisa, you stay in front of the mirror. Gaze steadily at yourself."

Leaving Natsunagi standing by the mirror, the two of us backed up a bit.

Then we waited for several minutes.

"Nothing's happening."

The big mirror showed Natsunagi's reflection, but that was all. There wasn't anything strange about it. Hel certainly didn't appear in the glass, and she wasn't going to. I was tired of waiting.

"Hey, SIESTA, what's the point of..." I'd just started to ask when SIESTA cut me off.

"It appears we need one more push."

She walked over to Natsunagi *and took the red ribbon out of her hair.*

"...!"

Instantly, the red eyes in the mirror widened dramatically.

Now that *the restraint of Siesta's ribbon* was gone, the figure reminded me of someone else. In the darkness, illuminated by the orange flame, Natsunagi's fingertips reached toward the mirror. "Another...me...?" she murmured. She sounded delirious.

Her right palm touched the glass. She squeezed her red eyes shut for a few seconds, then opened them again.

"Natsunagi?" I called, but she didn't turn around.

Instead—the Natsunagi in the mirror spoke to the one in front of us.

"It's been a long time, Master."

◆ An unknown tale of that day

"Is that Hel?"

The girl in the mirror had red eyes. Naturally, she still looked like Nagisa Natsunagi.

However, the reflection had greeted the one in front of the mirror as "Master."

That was what Hel had called Alicia—Natsunagi—last year. Meaning this one, the one talking, was...

"Is that the other me?" Natsunagi retreated a few steps, but she spoke to the mirror.

"That's right. I'm another you. My code name is Hel," the reflection told her. "Nothing but familiar faces here, I see." From beyond the glass, her gaze shifted to SIESTA and me, even though we were hanging back.

"There, you see? It's just like I told you. I said *you'd be my partner someday, Kimi.*"

She'd told me as much when she'd abducted me a year ago. Hel had claimed that her sacred text recorded the future, and that it said she and I would be partners.

Only—

"Sorry, but I'm your master's partner, not yours." I had no intention of doing whatever that so-called sacred text says. I'd told her as much plenty of times last year.

"You're as cold as ever." The figure in the mirror gave a faint smile.

Was this really the Hel I knew…? I stole a glance at SIESTA, but she was gazing straight ahead, expressionless.

"Well? You've gone to the trouble of summoning me after a year. What do you want?" The girl in the mirror narrowed her eyes. "Don't tell me… Are you planning to make me suffer more?" she asked Natsunagi sarcastically.

Hel was a second personality Natsunagi had created to escape the pain of SPES's experiments. She'd told us so a year ago, during that last fight. That was what had made her such a twisted, vicious person.

"No." Impulsively, I broke into their conversation. "There's something we want to ask you about what happened last year. About Siesta."

Hel had been a central figure in that string of Jack the Devil incidents, which meant she might have noticed something about Siesta's mistake. Or so I hoped, but…

"No idea." Hel shook her head in flat denial. "Anyway, thanks to that ace detective, it's impossible for me to get outside. She makes me utterly sick. Don't say that name where I can hear it ever again."

Hel glared at the left side of Natsunagi's chest with disgust.

"…In that case." Natsunagi gazed back at her reflection. "I'd like you to tell me about yourself instead."

Was this an attack from a different angle? First she'd encourage Hel to talk with her, then steer the conversation to that incident…or maybe to Siesta.

"You want to know about me? Ha-ha! A bit late for that." Hel's lips curled in a sneer, beyond the glass. "I don't have to tell you anything. And even if I did, I already said plenty during that fight a year ago. And look where that got me—sealed inside you… Or what? You want to laugh at me while I'm down?"

"No!" Natsunagi shouted at the mirror. "That's not what I'm talking about! I can't really learn anything about you from your mission or why you fight."

"…Then what about me do you want to know, Master?" Hel's eyebrows drew together; she looked a little bewildered.

"Um, well… Y-your hobbies, maybe?"

What is this, a marriage interview?

There, see? Hel looks completely appalled.

"—I really mean it, though." Natsunagi didn't back down. She gazed at the mirror, and her expression was serious again. "I want to know your favorite type of tea, for example, and whether you listen to pop music, and if you're the sort that takes long baths. *That's the you* I want to know. So…" She took a step toward to the mirror. "Tell me about yourself," she said. To her other self.

Oh, right. That's the kind of person Natsunagi is.

It was her passion talking. She'd never had a strategy. She genuinely wanted to have an actual conversation with her other personality. Nothing more.

"…Stupid." However, Hel promptly rejected Natsunagi's enthusiasm. "Besides, you should be the one who knows me best anyway."

"What do you mean?" Natsunagi tilted her head.

"You're the one who created me. Instead of asking me, it would be faster to just remember it."

Remember— Of course, Natsunagi might have seen those recorded memories from last year, but that didn't mean she'd reclaimed all eighteen years of her own memories. Up until now, she'd ceded lots of her memories and emotions to Hel, her other personality.

"But there's nothing Natsunagi can do about that now—"

"In that case..." Hel interrupted me. "If you're going to insist, I'll help you out a little. Let's retake my memories, and yours, together."

Then Hel's *red eyes glowed.*

"All right. *Go on and tell it in my place.* Tell your own story."

◆ Another past that must be told

Every morning when I woke up, I thought *This bed is way too hard.*

"My poor lower back..." I stretched, joints cracking and popping.

It couldn't be right to treat a growing girl like this. I couldn't actually complain, though. I had to be grateful that they were taking care of me at all.

"I'd better take my temperature."

That was the second thing I did every morning. As I slipped the thermometer into my pajama top, my eyes fell on the IV needle in my right hand. I was used to it, but seeing a needle sticking into me wasn't pleasant.

"So, 37.2 degrees Celsius."

My temperature was about what it always was, basically normal. I wrote it down, then climbed back into the hard bed to wait for breakfast. I'd lived like this for twelve whole years, ever since I was born.

I had a congenital heart disease, and I lived quietly in a hospital room. I couldn't go out and play with friends, and the only people who came to visit me were doctors on their rounds.

That was because I didn't have parents. From what I heard, they'd abandoned me soon after I was born. Yes, I was a tragic heroine, saddled with a backstory that even tearjerker dramas would turn down these days. All alone in the world, with an incurable illness. Right now, I was in a sickroom in a facility that took in kids who'd been discarded by their parents.

"Haaah, this sucks, huh?" I tried to comfort myself. Why was I the only one who had to go through stuff like this? "Arrrrgh... Maybe a prince will come and take me away."

Would he get me out of this hard bed and whisk me off to some distant country? ...And as fantasies went, was that one too cringey?

"Since I'm not a prince, should I come back some other time, Nagisa?"

Without warning, somebody called my name. When I looked in that direction, I saw a shape in the window... And this room was on the third floor. I smiled wryly. *Geez. I can't believe she does this every time.*
"Why are you ignoring me, hm?"
The figure slipped a strange tool in through the window, pried open the lock, and climbed into the room. Apparently I wasn't going to be able to pretend I hadn't noticed her.

"What do you want, Siesta?"

I shot the intruder a pointed glare.
"Here your friend's gone out of her way to visit you, and you're as cold as ever."
Siesta brought a round stool over from the corner and sat down by the bed, as if she did this all the time. I said the only people who came to visit me were doctors, but I'd forgotten the *troublemaking friends* I'd made lately.
One of them was Siesta. She had pale silver hair and blue eyes. I was one hundred percent Japanese, and I couldn't have been more jealous of her looks.
"Huh? Your face is kind of grubby."
There was a smudge of black soot on Siesta's cheek. Normally, her skin was so fair it gave her hair a run for its money.
"Oh, I was making a bomb and something went wrong, so I got dirty."
"You say that like you were making mud balls." *C'mon, it's still early in the morning. What is this kid doing?* "You shouldn't make bombs anymore."
I scolded Siesta with a sentence I was sure I'd never get to say again as long as I lived.
"But I might want to blow something up one day. Like a corporation."

"Well, you shouldn't do that either. No matter what your reasons are."
The last thing I wanted was a friend who got arrested for setting off a
bomb at her office because she hated her job.

"Well, *she's* the one who first suggested building bombs."

"Oh..."

I knew where this was going, but I didn't have to like it.

"Use my name already!"

Another girl, this one with long pink hair, poked her head through the
window after Siesta. She was as cute as a doll...but as you can tell, my
second bad friend wasn't at all ladylike.

"...Haaah. So you're here too, huh?"

As I looked at the pair, my shoulders slumped. Frankly, when these two
were in the same place, it got as noisy as a house party of Americans
who'd gotten together to watch football.

"Hey, what's that supposed to mean?! You're mean, *Nana!*" She clam-
bered down into the room and pummeled me lightly with her fists. Guess
that really rubbed her the wrong way

"The three of us are BFFs!"

"...We were, weren't we?"

"We *are*! Present tense! I write down what we did in my diary every
day!"

"Yes, yes, all right, *Ali.*"

These two were my recently acquired "bad friends," and they were
both really strange.

All the kids at this facility were good about doing what the adults told
them. I suspected it was because they had a nagging fear of being abandoned again. But these two were the odd ones out, making bombs and
climbing the walls to get into my hospital room, which was technically
off-limits. Seriously, they were shockingly weird.

"And why are you looking at us like we wear you out, Nagisa?" Siesta
shot me a cold, cross look.

"Oh, I was just thinking that kids are cute when they're a handful."

"...Of the three of us, I think I'm the most mature, you know."

"Nana, did you just say I was cute? Eh-heh-heh, lookit, look! This dress
is handmade!"

"I didn't mean it like that, and don't twirl around. I can see your panties."

"Wow, you're right. Then you twirl too, Sisi. We'll beat Nana with numbers that way."

"I want no part of that majority vote. And don't call me Sisi."

Our conversations always went like this. Somebody would say something dumb, and then somebody else would point out how dumb it was. Then we'd all crack up.

To me, that daily routine was—

"Excuse me." Just then, there was a knock at the door, and a man in his sixties entered. He was wearing a white lab coat. "How are you feeling... Well. You two are here too, I see."

The man was a doctor, and the director of this orphanage. As he noticed the other two, he gave a wry smile, although he knew that getting mad at them wouldn't do any good.

"*They* sent you this."

"...? Ooh!"

He'd handed me a new teddy bear. As far as gifts went, it did seem a little childish for me, but honestly, it was really cute.

"If I recall, they have a daughter who's about three years younger than you girls, so they may have had that age in mind."

The present was from a certain wealthy Japanese couple. From what I heard, they donated large amounts of money to this orphanage, and they also sent us gifts at regular intervals. I'd never met them, but the idea that they were thinking of us made me happy.

"Well? What did you need?" Siesta asked the doctor, rather suddenly. She seemed to know he hadn't come here just to give me a present.

"...I'm no match for you, am I." The doctor gave another bitter smile. "Actually, I'd like all three of you to give me a little help before breakfast today. It has to be done on an empty stomach."

"I see. All right."

Siesta nodded, without attempting to fight; it wouldn't have done any good anyway.

Ali planted her hands on her hips and said, "If I *must*," as if she was used to it. But as for me...

"You look pretty reluctant." The doctor glanced at me. He sounded troubled. We had this exchange every single time. But I didn't care what he said to me; this was something I just couldn't—

"This will benefit you kids as well, you know. You understand that, don't you?"

"...Yes."

Oh, I understood, all right. In the end, I always had to do what the adults said.

"Thank you for your cooperation—Number 602."

With a satisfied smile at doing what he came to do, the doctor turned to leave the room. "You got it wrong," I called after him. I had to say something. "My name isn't Number 602. It's Nagisa."

Nagisa. That was the name Siesta had given me.

They only called me by a number here, but she'd given me a name.

"...Yes, that's right." The doctor looked back again, smiled gently, and left.

"Nagisa..." Siesta was gazing at me as if she wanted to say something.

"Yes, I know."

Thinking of the painful hours that lay ahead, I nodded.

The "help" the doctor was referring to had to do with the *medication trials* this facility conducted.

The orphanage's operating costs were covered by using the children as clinical trial subjects.

◆ Almost like a detective

The medication trials were conducted once every two weeks or so.

The facility's several dozen children were the test subjects, and even though I had a weak heart, I wasn't exempted. They made me participate every time. They said there was data they could get precisely because I wasn't healthy, but that did mean the burden on me was greater than it was for the others.

The trials had a lot of side effects; we'd come down with fevers, throw up, or even develop burning pain all over. Still, our hard work helped keep the facility going...and the sense of mission, the idea that they were helping create medicines for unknown diseases, kept the children going.

I had one more special reason to work hard: my troublemaking friends.

First, there was Siesta. We'd made friends a few months ago; before that, I'd always been on my own. I didn't know which facility had sent her here, or even what country she was from. I tended to get depressed, though, and she'd come to play and talk with me almost every day.

Then, through her, I'd met another friend.

"I found something funny," Siesta had said when she brought Ali to me one day. Almost as if she were bringing me a new toy. She hadn't been wrong, though: When I was with her, I really never got bored...and although I might complain, I always looked forward to the days when they came to visit.

—And yet.

"Why aren't they coming?"

The last time I'd seen them was on the day of the clinical trial. For one day, three days, a week after that, they hadn't come to my room at all. Had I made them mad somehow? Or had something happened to them?

"...Where did they go?"

All I could do was wait for them to come to my room again. I was lonely, but I'd just have to deal. I'd been on my own all along anyway.

Besides, I'd fought with Siesta a lot. Maybe it was better this way. Yes, I was lonely, but there was no way around it.

...Am I lonely?

I was disgusted with myself for being so spoiled. I wanted to throw my whole revolting self away.

Arrrgh, I wish someone would just take over for me.

"Haaaaah." I heaved a big sigh that nobody else would ever hear.

"People say that every time you sigh, it delays your marriage by a year." Siesta poked her head out from under my bed.

"Yaaaaaaaaaaaaaaaaaaugh!"

On reflex, I hurled the teddy bear at her.

"Hey, don't yell. They'll catch me."

"Dangerous characters like you *should* get caught, and fast!"

Th-that scared me! I thought my heart might stop. *Did she forget I've got a bad heart? I really wish she'd give me a break...*

"Were you lonely?"

"...Not particularly. I haven't been alone in a long time. I was trying to enjoy it."

I got back into bed, hoping to shut down any further questions from Siesta. Times like these, the best policy was to look at the patterns on the ceiling and ignore her.

"Lying delays your marriage, you know."

This time, a section of the ceiling opened up and Ali's face appeared.

"Yaaaaaaaaaaaaaaaaaaaaaaaugh! Are you actually trying to give me a heart attack?!"

I also wished they'd stop spouting weird theories I'd never heard of. How long did they want to keep me single, anyway?

"Actually, I had something kinda serious to discuss." Siesta crawled out from under the bed, then sat down on a stool at my bedside.

"Huh? Where's my chair?" Ali asked from the ceiling.

"You just lie on your stomach up there and wait."

"Sisi, you're being so mean to me."

Without sparing a glance for Ali, Siesta turned to me. "It's been three months since I came to this facility, and I'm starting to get concerned about something." For some reason, she glanced around the room. Then she picked up the teddy bear I'd hurled at her a minute ago. "I've been wondering why they have to run clinical trials when they get donations."

She was getting suspicious of the explanation that the facility relied on money from the trials to cover its operating expenses. She had a point. If this place was using its children as guinea pigs to earn extra money, that was a problem. We didn't want to help with those trials. We only put up with them to protect the life we knew.

"Besides, look."

There was a zipper in the teddy bear's back. Siesta unzipped it, and something fell out. My eyes widened.

There was a little machine on the floor that looked like a round battery.

"It's a bug," Ali said from the ceiling, her chin resting in her hands. "The facility's hiding something from us."

"...! You mean they're watching us? Then aren't they listening to us right now...?" I worried.

"It's all right," Siesta told me. "I made sure they'll hear a dummy audio track from this room, instead of what we say."

"Wait just a minute! When did I wander into a spy movie?!"

"That's part of the reason we haven't come to visit for a week. We were getting ready. I'm sorry."

"Getting ready for what?! And also how?!"

Haaah, I can't find comebacks fast enough. Couldn't they be a little more considerate of my physical limitations here?

...Hm? Be considerate of my limitations?

"Did you do this for me?"

Why had Siesta developed suspicions about the facility and made her move now? Could it be because she'd seen how reluctant I was to help with that trial the other day?

"I don't know what you mean." Siesta got to her feet smoothly, acting as if she hadn't noticed a thing. "I just want to find out what this place is hiding." Her eyes seemed to be focused on something far away.

"...Heh-heh." I laughed a little behind her.

"I don't recall saying anything funny." Siesta seemed to think I was mocking her, and she turned around with a sulky face I never saw from her.

"No, that's not it." I smiled and shook my head. It was just that, when I'd seen Siesta, I'd thought...

"You seem like a detective."

"All right, Sisi. Do it."

"Copy that. Here we go!" Siesta pulled me onto her back for some unfathomable reason, following Ali's instructions.

"Huh? What?! What—what—what's this...?"

"Starting now, you're going to be in on this with us, Nagisa." As usual, Siesta opened the window. Then she set a foot on the sill.

"Whoa, wait-wait-wait! Wait, okay? What are you going to do?!" I had a really, truly, horribly bad feeling about this…but by then, I had no other options.

Because, with me on her back, Siesta had already—jumped.

"It's fine. My shoes can run through thin air."

"That's impossibleeeeeeeeee!"

I squeezed my eyes shut, sure I was about to die.

◆ Girls dream of secret bases, too

"Hm. It looks like she's awake."

That was Siesta's voice. When I opened my eyes, her beautiful face was the first thing I saw.

Had I passed out after that? I was lying on a sofa. When I sat up, I realized I was in an unfamiliar room.

"Welcome to our secret base!"

That was Ali. When I turned toward her voice, she was standing there triumphantly, hands on her hips.

"Secret base?"

I looked around and noticed that the room was a little odd.

"Is this all cardboard…?"

The whole place—walls, table, and even the sofa I was lying on—was made of cardboard. It was a cardboard house.

It did seem about as secret-basey as it could possibly be. The question was what they did in it, and why they'd brought me here.

"This is our strategy HQ." Siesta sat down on a cardboard chair. I noticed the plural, meaning our other troublemaking friend was involved. Of course.

"She asked me to make this, so I did. Sisi, I swear… Once she sets her mind to something, she just doesn't stop." Ali turned her palms to the ceiling in an exaggerated shrug of resignation.

"…I really wish you wouldn't call me by that silly nickname."

Siesta looked away; she seemed unusually embarrassed. She always acted very grown-up, and it was a relief to see that she had a childish side as well.

"So you said this was a strategy HQ?"

"That's right. We've made this the base for our resistance while we put together a strategy to strike back against the adults."

Siesta opened the doors of a cardboard closet. Inside were...

"What...are those...?"

They were weapons. Lots of them. The sort I'd only seen in fiction. I didn't know their technical names, but there were all kinds of guns and blades of various shapes in there. *Don't tell me these were the work of...*

"Eh-heh-heh! I made them!" Ali flashed me a peace sign.

I'd expect no less from a little girl who made bombs for fun. Ali made all sorts of toys, calling them "inventions," so the other kids adored her. I'd never dreamed she'd made anything this crazy, though...

"But do we really need things like this?" I eyed the weapons from a safe distance. I didn't even have the courage to touch them. "If you have something this dangerous on hand, you mean you're planning to fight the adults for real, right?"

And really, was there any need to "resist" this much? What were the adults, and this facility, hiding from us?

"Good question. We don't know yet." Siesta shook her head quietly. "There's no harm in being prepared for anything, though. We should try to resolve trouble before it even comes up."

"...Y-you're getting all complicated on me."

Is she really my age? Well, I mean, she's never told me her actual age, but...

"So what do you think?" Siesta asked. "Will you fight alongside us, Nagisa?"

To be honest, I was scared.

Not of defying the adults, though—of learning the truth. I was just scared that something was going to change irreversibly.

It wasn't that I was content with this place, of course. If finding out the truth would free us from those awful clinical trials, I couldn't even tell you how good it would be.

But these past twelve years—my whole life— I'd been here, in that hospital bed. No matter what I did, that time grabbed my legs and refused to let go.

"I..."

I couldn't find an answer right away, and I lowered my eyes.

Watching me, Siesta said, "Someday, let's just walk out there and look at the ocean in broad daylight." That made me remember our first meeting. And then: "Let's fix your heart, too. Then we'll run around at the waterline all we want. But if we're going to have a future like that—something has to change." She held her left hand out to me.

"...I guess it's not much of a choice." Giving a weary, dramatic sigh, I said, "I'll help you!" I took her hand and got to my feet.

"...Hrm. Why are you two off in your own little world over there?"

One of us seemed to be in a bad mood. Ali had her arms crossed and was standing tall—well, maybe not *that* tall—watching us.

"Don't be cranky. I'll give you a big hug later. Or at least Nagisa will."

"Sisi, you dummy! Naaaanaaaaa!"

"Whoa, you smell like oil..."

"I was just making an inveeentiooon!"

As we watched Ali throw her tantrum, we both laughed.

If it was the three of us. If it was us, we'd be able to get over any changes, any hardship.

Somewhere along the way, all my reluctance had evaporated.

"All right, once again..." I moved so that the three of us were standing in a circle. "Let's uncover this facility's secret together!" I held my right hand out toward the other two, palm down.

"Huh? Oh. We're doing this, hm?"

"Ah-ha-ha! Nana, you're more of a little kid than I thought."

"Don't yank the rug out from under me right at the end!"

We laughed, and got mad, and cheered, and made our vow together.

"...Geez." How could I have embarrassed myself like that? Unbelievable. I went back to the sofa by myself, propped my elbow on its arm, and rested my chin in my hand.

"Hm?"

When I took another look around the room, I realized there were a whole bunch of toys and stuffed animals over by the window. Were they the ones that couple always gave us? Even then, it seemed like too many for Ali to have gotten on her own.

Well, about all I could say now was…

"I think you're a hundred times more of a kid than I am, Ali."

◆ The real enemy

Several weeks later…

"Ow! Siesta, you just stepped on my foot."

Siesta and I were walking through a dark building, side by side.

"Huh? No I didn't."

"…You're kidding me. Then what just…"

It was so dark. A sudden chill ran down my spine, and I caught Siesta's arm.

"Yes, I'm kidding."

"That's just mean! Why would you do that?!" I swear, this girl… You'd think she was born just to tease people. I really couldn't handle her, and I prayed fervently that someday she'd find somebody who could take over for me.

"And? Is the *enemy* really this way?" I asked, lowering my voice.

"Yes, definitely. All the cameras in the building are currently under our control."

We'd remotely hijacked the surveillance cameras, and we knew exactly who was in the building and where. Ali was keeping an eye on the situation and giving us directions. She was back in the strategy HQ, watching over us to make sure nothing went wrong.

"This is finally it," I said, psyching myself up.

"This is our answer," said Siesta. "We won't do as we're told anymore."

"…Right."

For the past few weeks, we'd investigated this facility under Siesta's leadership. We'd taken sneaky pictures, placed wiretaps, and done all kinds of recon. We'd used Ali's inventions to gather information until finally we made our big discovery. Today, Siesta and I were going to confront the enemy with it.

Of course, that was going to change the way we lived.

Because I was physically fragile, I'd hardly ever played with friends. Lately, though, I'd made two friends I could count as partners in crime. If we turned this facility against us, we might get split up. And I couldn't deny that idea made me feel a little lonely.

"Do you want to back out?" Siesta whispered sweetly, as if she'd read my mind.

"You're such a jerk." I let her have it. Really I just needed to get the thought out of my head.

Yes, I'd hesitated. I'd thought maybe it would be better to leave this to the other two. If I ran now, though, I was sure I'd regret it later.

This is my chance, I thought. My very last chance to fly away from that hard bed. From this birdcage.

And so I—

"I'm doing it. I won't forgive you two if you leave me out of this."

As I spoke, I slipped my hand into my pocket, and my fingers touched something hard. *I really hope I don't have to use this.*

"Honestly. You're both such children." Siesta smiled gently.

After we'd walked a little farther, we reached our destination. It was an elevator that led to the basement. We nodded to each other, stepped in, and went down.

When the doors opened, the first thing we saw was several big tanks. They were filled with green liquid, and there was *something* inside them, hooked up to tubes.

"Well, well. Visitors?"

A voice spoke from somewhere near the back of the room.

"It's a little too soon for the experiment, though."

The speaker stepped into view—a bespectacled man in a white lab coat: my doctor, and the director of the orphanage.

"Are those *pseudohumans*?"

Siesta pointed at the contents of the enormous tanks.

"...Oh-ho. You've done your homework." The corners of his lips rose, silently acknowledging that Siesta's hypothesis was correct.

That was the secret of this facility.

Those weren't actually clinical trials. They were human experimentation.

It was an attempt to grant extraordinary physical abilities by implanting a certain unknown energy source in human bodies. They were conducting this experiment on children who had no families, over and over, with the goal of eventually creating a "pseudohuman."

"Is that what you are, too?" Siesta pressed the director.

"I am Seed."

Suddenly, the man's tone changed. At the same time, his appearance shifted through several different stages. First he was a blond man with his hair combed back, and then his body distorted into a voluptuous woman with long hair. Then, finally—

"This is the form I'm most accustomed to now."

He transformed into a slim young man with white hair.

Well, I couldn't tell whether he was actually male. His symmetrical features could have been feminine as well, if you wanted to see it that way... I'm not sure how to put it. There was something almost holy about that lack of gender, that total androgyny.

"That said, it is just a temporary shape. The ones in there are also not the real thing." The youth who'd called himself Seed gazed at the contents of the tanks with clear eyes. "They're copies I created from pieces of myself."

"Then you're trying to use the children to make a real pseudohuman?"

"Well, for now, that's accurate in a general way," Seed replied. "Although I'm not partial to the word *pseudohuman.*"

"What for?" Without thinking, I broke into their conversation. "Is it for war? Money? ...Why did you have to sacrifice us?"

I'd lived at the facility for twelve years, but there was something I'd never realized.

Many of the children had disappeared.

Kids who'd been right next to me during a clinical trial one day had been gone the next. They must have died during the experiments... and then our memories of them had been erased with some sort of drug.

"Some try to use my power to gain money or military might. However, personally, I don't have the slightest interest in them. The only thing that motivates me—is a tenacious instinct for survival." Seed's face was expressionless. Swaying lightly, he blocked our way. "Well? What now? You've learned the truth of this facility, and my objectives. What's the point of confronting me?"

"We'll stop you, of course. No matter what it takes."

In the next moment, Siesta had taken the musket from her back and pointed it at him. It was another of Ali's inventions, naturally.

"An empty threat?"

"It's real." As I spoke, I took a detonator switch out of my pocket.

This facility stood on an isolated island, far out in the ocean. We knew we couldn't run, so we'd have to fight. "All I have to do is push this button, and I'll blow the laboratory to bits."

I moved my thumb toward the red button. If I pushed it, we wouldn't escape unscathed either, but it should make for a decent negotiating tactic.

"—You really are still green." Something like disappointment flashed across Seed's blank face. "The plan begins now, though."

"Wh-what are you talking about?!"

He wasn't taking us seriously at all. I held the switch out one more time, making sure he'd seen it.

"You'd sacrifice yourself, hm? It's no use. I can tell from one look at your trembling fingers that you aren't brave enough to push it."

"I—!"

Just as I was about to argue back...

"Then *why not push it?*"

...Seed's eyes flared red.

"...Huh?"

For some reason, my thumb moved on its own. It was being drawn toward the button. "Wait, wait-wait! What?! No...!"

My thumb was going to press the switch. And I knew this bomb was real…

"—!" Noticing the emergency, Siesta pointed her gun at Seed and pulled the trigger.

"…? It…didn't fire?"

No bullet came from the muzzle. And in the meantime, my thumb had pressed the red button, but—

"Nothing's happening?"

At first glance, it looked as though we'd been saved, but it did mean we had another big problem.

Both of Ali's inventions were duds.

Was it coincidence? Just bad luck? Or…

"I've known of this future ever since the distant past," Seed murmured. And then…

"Ooh, you two are being so bad."

Someone else spoke behind us.

Fearfully, I turned around to see a girl with pink hair.

"You can't point those weapons at my boss."

◆ The last name I called was…

"Ali…?"

I couldn't accept what I was seeing, and I fumbled and dropped the detonator switch. Ali passed right by me and went to stand beside Seed. She was smiling faintly.

"Why are you…?"

Next to me, Siesta was watching her too. Her expression was grim, and her eyes were narrowed. I was sure she was praying that the explanation she'd just thought of was incorrect.

"Ah-ha-ha! So sorry. I've been on his side the whole time," Ali said, forcing us to face the cruel reality. "I've known kids were disappearing from the facility for ages."

That was something we'd only found out recently—the deaths of the children involved in failed experiments and the drugs to erase them from our memories.

But Ali said, "I've kept a journal for years and years; I've never missed a day. When I compared my faulty memories to it, I realized that kids were vanishing and nobody knew."

Come to think of it, Ali's secret base had so many dolls and stuffed animals in it that I hadn't been able to believe they were all hers. Had those belonged to the kids who'd died? Apparently, she really had known about the disappearances long before we found out.

"...If you knew that, then why did you join them?"

She should be able to see who the bad guys were here.

"Well, it's only natural to side with whoever's strongest, isn't it?" Ali had used similar reasoning to reach a completely different conclusion. "You have to live smart, you know." She gave us a teasing smile. "Anyway, these kids won't do at all." Her attitude changed abruptly, and she pointed at Siesta and me as she advised Seed. "Any girl this easy to fool won't be any use to you. Don't waste seeds on them."

Seeds? I hadn't heard that term before.

However, from what we'd learned so far and the direction the conversation was heading, I could guess. "Seeds" must be the unknown energy source that was supposed to turn children into pseudohumans. Ali was saying Siesta and I shouldn't be allowed to have them.

"You should give me one instead, please," she said, trying to persuade Seed that she was worthy. "As an inventor, I'm gonna be interested in pseudohumans. Obviously. Besides, I've given you all this help. Okay? C'mon, won't you?"

She sounded exactly like the childish Ali I knew as she pestered Seed for the seed like a spoiled little brat.

—But.

"I think it's too early for you." Seed rejected her proposal, still blank-faced.

"It's fine." I didn't know why she was being so stubborn, but she doubled down on her request. "It's fine, I know I can handle it. I'll master the seed for sure."

"Then what shall we do with these two?" Seed asked, almost as if he was testing her.

"These two" were me and Siesta, of course. We'd learned the secret of this facility and what Seed really was, and he was asking *how to dispose of us.*

"Just take some of their memories, the way you always do," Ali replied. "After that, you can let them go. I really don't think they'll be useful anyway." She kept on talking a blue streak, without sparing a glance for us. "Oh, right, make them forget me too, would you? Kinda gross to think about them remembering me the whole time."

...*Oh, is* that *what this is,* I thought.

Ali was Ali after all.

"Also, while we're at it, I doubt we need the other kids either. I mean, you were using this place to create a pseudohuman, right? If I become your first success, you won't need this lab anymore—"

While Ali was still chattering away, Siesta interrupted.

"Are you really okay with that?"

Her voice was very sharp.

"To summarize what I just heard, you're planning to sacrifice yourself to save us."

"...!"

For the first time, Ali's face twisted.

That's right. I'd had the wrong idea. When something you believed in turns out to be wrong, you have to ask yourself what you're going to believe in again. I should have trusted Ali's emotions instead of her actions. I should have trusted her nature, the same way I always had.

"...This is fine," Ali murmured quietly. "If somebody's sacrificed, this experiment will end. If I master the seed properly, no one else has to go through this again! Isn't that right?!"

Ali had only been pretending to be Seed's ally, in order to protect us. She'd picked up on the facility's secret before anyone else, and I'm sure she'd initially planned to do something about it on her own...but then Siesta had begun doing the same thing.

And Ali knew that once Siesta set her mind to something, she wouldn't stop. She'd pulled us into this, but at the same time, she'd acted as a double agent to keep us safe.

"So please…" Laying a hand on her chest, Ali shouted at Seed, "I'll do it! I'll inherit that seed for you! So these two can be—"

"Fine." Seed, whose face was still expressionless, accepted her plea. The next moment, *a single, long tentacle sprouted* from his back.

"…! I won't let you do it!"

Something supernatural was playing out right in front of me, and I almost cringed back. But the tip of that tentacle was sharp, and it was easy to imagine what was about to happen. Even though I had no weapon, I ran to Ali.

"…!"

But that was when a terrible pain shot through the left side of my chest. My heart… *Not now!*

"Nagisa!"

"G…go…" I'd crouched down. Siesta was focused on me, but with a glance, I told her to go to Ali.

—But then.

"This is a prime opportunity for an experiment. We can't have you obstructing it."

Even though none of us had spoken, we heard a voice.

"…!"

Almost immediately, Siesta crashed to the floor. It was as if something had fallen on her.

"Come on, no struggling."

"! No… Don't…!" Siesta's back arched. Her voice was trembling.

"Ha-ha! Do you like the feel of my tongue that much?" Unpleasant laughter echoed from the empty air. Our opponent must have made himself invisible. Even Siesta hadn't predicted a being who wouldn't show up on a security camera.

We were powerless. In front of us was an enormous enemy with a tentacle that moved as if it had a life of its own, and one solitary girl.

"All right. Let us conduct the last experiment," Seed said evenly. "This is my seed. Accept it."

The pointed tentacle closed in on Ali's chest, over her heart. It was the worst possible way this could end.

She twisted halfway around, calling back to us. She was wearing her usual artless smile.

"Hurry up and forget me."

I don't have any clear memories of what happened after that.

Was the shock so great that I lost them?

Or did I force that pain and suffering *onto someone else*?

It was as if I'd been locked up in the dark. I lost all sense of myself as a person.

At the end, I screamed a name.

My friend wasn't compatible with the seed. She died in a welter of blood right there in front of me. Only her name was etched in my mind forever.

"—Alicia!"

◆ Finding mistakes and comparing answers

"That's right. Six years ago, the three of us fought SPES at that facility on the island. The ace detective...well, Siesta, and me, and Alicia." Natsunagi said all of that in a rush, as if it was flooding back to her.

One year ago, Charlie and I had encountered the enemy leader at a laboratory. That had to be the test facility that had come up in the story. Six years ago, SPES had been attempting to create pseudohumans there, using children as guinea pigs.

That story had given us two new pieces of information.

The first was that Siesta and Natsunagi had known each other as kids.

Siesta hadn't initially given her the name "Nagisa" last year, just before she died, but six years ago. Had she given her that name again, five years later, because she'd realized Hel was actually her former friend Nagisa?

And the other fact was—

"Alicia actually existed. She wasn't just part of Natsunagi."

One year ago, when I'd met Alicia in London, I'd assumed that her appearance was *made up*, something Hel (or Natsunagi) had created with *Cerberus's seed*. There had been a real Alicia, though—a girl with pink hair. Natsunagi had met her at the facility six years ago. Then she'd seen her die. The image of her must have been indelibly imprinted on her mind, and when she used Cerberus's seed several years later, she'd unconsciously assumed her appearance. Then, even though she'd lost her memories, the name Alicia had still been somewhere in her mind.

"I never once called my master 'Alicia,' you know." In the mirror, Hel narrowed her eyes.

She was right. Hel had kept all of Natsunagi's memories in her place. She had to have known that "Alicia" was someone else.

"Still. I suppose you can't even imagine it, but there was a time when that ace detective was young and inexperienced," Hel went on.

Siesta had still been a child, and she'd gone up against Seed without a plan. Chameleon alone had been too much for her. Maybe it was those experiences that had molded her into the flawless ace detective I knew.

Even so…

"By last year, Siesta wasn't the type of person who'd fail easily. Why didn't she notice that Natsunagi looked like Alicia in London? Why didn't she notice something was off?"

Siesta, Alicia, and Natsunagi had met six years ago. Five years couldn't have been enough to make Siesta forget her friends. I really couldn't imagine that she'd see those pink ponytails and not realize it was Alicia.

"It's simple," Hel said. "The ace detective was missing memories as well."

"…! Siesta? Missing memories?"

Well, actually, that made sense. Natsunagi had just told us about it herself: At that test facility, the children's memories had been erased on a regular basis. After Alicia's death, Siesta must have been forced to forget some of her memories from the facility, including SPES, Natsunagi, and Alicia.

"What happened to Siesta after that?"

"She fled the island." Hel gave a cold smile. "Even after they'd partially erased her memories of SPES and her friends, that ace detective slipped out of the facility... She wasn't running away, though. She did it to fight. She stole Seed's seed, and one day, without warning, she was gone."

"Siesta took a seed?"

Maybe that shouldn't have surprised me. Siesta's combat abilities were superhuman. And then there was her heart...

Just like Bat's ears, Chameleon's tongue, and Cerberus's nose, Siesta's heart had had a special ability. When Natsunagi had acquired the heart, she'd picked up her memories as well. Maybe that had been due to the seed's power.

"...Why?" I couldn't wait for Hel to continue her explanation. "If Siesta's memories had been erased, then why did she steal the seed and escape from the orphanage?"

"You're going to make me say it? Me, your enemy?" In the mirror, her lips twisted. "It's simple. Even if she forgot why she was fighting, or who her enemy was, she remembered the mission she'd been given. That's all," she said with a bitter, dissatisfied smile. "All right. I think I've told you most of what there is to know about the past. You certainly have it rough, dredging up stories that are over and done with from a year ago, or four years, or six."

...She had a point. Natsunagi, Siesta, and I had forgotten all sorts of things, and they were all vital memories. Lately we'd been spending most of our time gathering the fragments of them, one by one.

This settling of accounts with the past must have started on that day.

The day when Nagisa Natsunagi woke me up, in that classroom after school.

The day when she'd set this story in motion again after it should have ended.

This story in which the detective was dead.

"Nagisa." Siesta took a step forward and finally spoke to Natsunagi's back. "Are you sure it's all right to end this story this way?"

Those blue eyes were unwavering. Even as part of a mechanical doll, they hadn't changed. I knew this gaze—it was the one directed at me a year ago, when I'd guessed that Hel and Alicia were the same person and then tried to pretend it wasn't true. She wouldn't let you lie or run away.

"Hel."

Acknowledging those feelings, Natsunagi spoke to her reflection in the mirror.

"What happened to me after that? After I saw Alicia die."

Natsunagi's story hadn't ended yet.

Alicia had died, Siesta had escaped from the facility...but what had happened to Nagisa Natsunagi?

"That's when I was born," Hel told her.

This tale had begun when Natsunagi said she wanted to know more about Hel; it would end with her, too.

"Well, my consciousness was already inside you, dormant. To be more accurate, that was the first time I became your dominant personality, Master."

And ever since then, Natsunagi's body had been under Hel's control? The shock of Alicia's death had destabilized her memories and personality, and Hel had seized her chance.

"After that, I became a formal member of SPES. I didn't mind letting them experiment on me. The other children were in the way, and I ran them all out of the facility. After that, I was special to Father, his one and only."

Was that what had happened...? Then Siesta and I had encountered Hel in London last year, after she'd risen through the ranks to become one of SPES's officers.

...Still, there was something in that explanation that just didn't ring true for me.

"Why would you go that far for SPES? For Seed?"

Seed had said it was his survival instinct that was making him attack humanity. Since SPES's officers were all clones of him, they were cooperating because that was what their instincts demanded.

Hel was different, though. She was human, and she was also an acquired personality that had grown in Natsunagi's mind. There was no logical reason for her to align herself with Seed.

"Heh. Are you a sadist?" The red eyes in the mirror narrowed. "Look, don't make me embarrass myself over and over. —It was love, all right? Love." The girl gave a self-deprecating smile. "That was the core I needed."

"The core...?"

"That's right. You could call it a tether, there to keep me in this world. Without it, I felt as if I'd disappear. I am just a fake, after all."

Oddly enough, her master Natsunagi had confessed to having the exact same worry. She'd been suffering after she'd lost her memories and identity too. However, the pain had been the same for Hel. As an alternate personality who had no physical body, she was an extremely vague concept.

"Will you laugh at me for seeking love for such a reason? For sidling up to Father and trying to win his affection because I didn't want to disappear? For blindly believing in his love, and deceiving my comrades, and tormenting innocents? For losing the battle and losing my power after all I'd done? —Will you laugh?" she asked us, smiling.

"No. I won't," said Natsunagi.

"How could I?" she continued. "More importantly, I'm sorry. And thank you."

"...What are you saying?" Hel hadn't been expecting to hear that from Natsunagi, and she grimaced.

"First, the things I was never able to say to you directly. You shouldered all my pain and suffering, didn't you? I'm sorry... I'm so sorry."

Hel was an alternate personality Natsunagi had unknowingly created to help herself escape her pain. In a way, she'd been born just to take over someone else's suffering. Now, Natsunagi was telling this other self what she felt for the very first time.

"'Thank you'? I—I don't want thanks from—!"

"Well, I mean..." Before Hel could work herself into a rage, Natsunagi spoke to her from the heart. "You protected me."

"From pain and hardship, you mean? I really don't want the person I had to shield thanking me."

"No, not that." Rejecting Hel's assumptions again, Natsunagi gazed into the mirror.

"You became a member of SPES *in order to protect me.* Didn't you?"

◆ There are no monsters anymore

"I don't know what you're talking about." Hel's lip curled. "I joined SPES for your sake? That can't possibly be—"

"I mean, if you hadn't, they would have killed me."

"…!"

The reflection's expression slipped—more like shattered, really.

"Six years ago, we learned SPES's secret. Alicia wasn't able to take the seed, and she was killed. My body was too frail to be of use to SPES. They would have killed me too, before long. They should have. But then you appeared."

Natsunagi looked steadily at her other self in the mirror.

"Hel, by insisting that you could be useful to SPES, you kept them from disposing of me. When you swore loyalty to Seed, you were trying to save my life. It was all for my sake. In order to protect me, you became a devil."

"…! You can't prove any of that. What proof do you have that I'm that soft?" Hel was breathing roughly.

"You said it yourself. *You let the facility's children get away.*" Natsunagi hadn't let a single word Hel said slip past her. She went on building her theory. "You said you intended to make yourself special to Seed, but that's not convincing. You have a heart. You can feel sympathy for others."

"A human heart? …That's impossible. You know how many innocent people I killed in London."

"You're right. And it's not a minor crime. But you did that to save me, too."

"…!" Hel's red eyes widened.

"One year ago, in the fight with Siesta, you lost your heart. That meant my body would die."

It had happened right after the battle between the humanoid weapon and the biological weapon in London. Using her *hand mirror*, Siesta had turned Hel's red eyes against her, and Hel had run her own heart through with her sword. Not only had it been a life-or-death crisis for Hel, but it should have meant death for her master. "After Cerberus died, you made it look as if you were continuing his Jack the Devil killings…but you were actually searching for a compatible heart for me."

"…! But the ace detective didn't say a word about that last year. She thought I'd just been running through hearts like batteries in an attempt to keep myself alive. Are you saying she was wrong, Master?" Hel pressed Natsunagi about her intentions, her eyes dark.

"No. Siesta herself is saying that she came to the wrong conclusion."

"…Oh," I murmured. That was the mistake SIESTA had asked us to find, the mistake Siesta had made a year ago.

Siesta had misread Hel's motives—*misread her emotions.*

"The ace detective said that? Don't make me laugh. When would she have—" Before she could finish her sentence, Hel froze.

"You understand, don't you? You're me, after all," Natsunagi reasoned. "Siesta lives in me. Over this past year, she's been talking with your personality in my subconscious. During that time, she came to the conclusion I just stated. She realized that as far as you're concerned, I'm actually the most important thing in the world."

"…!"

The eyes of the girl in the mirror wavered as if she felt unsettled.

"Hel. Most people would accuse you of being a devil who took innocent lives. I know, though. I'm the only one who does. Even if you are a devil… you're definitely not *a monster with no feelings.*" Natsunagi refused to accept Hel's mocking self-evaluation. "You said you wanted to be loved, and maybe that's true. But you didn't just want to be loved. You loved me. You were kind enough to love me."

"Stop…!" Hel's heartrending scream echoed in the quiet room, where only the flame of the lantern flickered.

Natsunagi didn't stop. "Your sins are mine. I know I'll pay for them someday."

"Stop it… I don't… I didn't want that…"

A single tear trickled down the face of the girl in the mirror.

Was it Natsunagi's, or…?

As an outsider, I had no way of knowing. I had no right to make conjectures, either.

—Even so.

"No. I'll help you carry your sins. We'll spend our whole lives atoning for them. After all—" Natsunagi held her palm up to the mirror.

"There's no such thing as only taking, or only giving. No relationship is that one-sided. Am I wrong?"

This was a mirror. An infinity mirror bringing two girls to face each other.

Everything went both ways—sins, love, tears, and even smiles.

If Natsunagi believed in Hel, then I was sure—

"I swear—you're such a fool, Master," the girl in the mirror whispered.

In the next moment, I heard it. I saw it plainly.

The big mirror cracked loudly, and Hel leaped out of it. Natsunagi caught her and held her close.

"Thank you."

I'm sure that was the moment Nagisa Natsunagi graduated from her past.

◆ And so a new case file begins

"So? Exactly what kind of story was that?"

The conversation in front of the mirror was over, and SIESTA and I were talking in the living room.

Immediately after that, Natsunagi had passed out; Siesta had said it was probably a reaction to suddenly regaining her memories. Right now, she was resting in the bedroom.

"What do you mean, 'what kind of story'?" Siesta asked, elegantly sipping her tea. Apparently, androids needed to rehydrate too.

"Don't play dumb. When you said you'd summon Hel with an infinity mirror, you were lying, right?"

I know those urban legends about infinity mirrors—about how you could summon devils with them, or see the past and the future. We'd summoned Natsunagi's alternate personality into the mirror and asked her about the past, but I just couldn't make it feel real.

"You're as hardheaded as ever, Kimihiko." She set her cup in its saucer. Her expression and posture were identical to the real detective's. "Although you're also correct."

"I am, huh?"

Then why did you call me names?

"That said, Nagisa actually was talking with Hel."

"You mean she was playing both roles in that conversation?"

No, "role" probably wasn't the right word here. It was more as if she'd been talking with herself, through the mirror.

"I only prepared a place where that could occur easily. After that, Nagisa summoned Hel from her subconscious and had a talk with her."

"I see… So in a sense, Hel was actually there?"

Two girls, separated by a mirror.

Natsunagi and Hel had definitely met there, confronted each other, and talked things out.

I was sure Natsunagi had regained all her memories now, in the truest sense. At this point, she'd be able to accept their reality and move forward.

"By the way." I decided to ask about something that had been bothering me. "If Siesta realized she'd made a mistake during the past year, how did she tell you about it?"

If Siesta had asked us to find the error, Siesta must have told her about it somehow. However, Siesta had apparently noticed her mistake while talking with Hel inside Natsunagi's body.

Since Siesta's own body was gone, how had she passed the message on to SIESTA?

In response to these perfectly natural questions, SIESTA said, "It happened the one time Mistress Siesta borrowed Nagisa's body." She began to talk about last week's incident. "Immediately after your fight with Chameleon on that cruise ship, Mistress Siesta instructed me to contact your group."

"...Ah. It happened while I was out cold, then."

So that was when she'd done it. After she'd gotten all of her business out of the way, Siesta had gone back to sleep inside Natsunagi.

"Still, who'd have thought Siesta would deduce wrong?"

I wasn't trying to criticize her. I was just genuinely startled.

"That may have been due to her missing memories as well." SIESTA's voice was quiet; she gazed into her cup. "Mistress Siesta had forgotten both Alicia and Nagisa. She didn't remember how Hel's personality had been created. However, if she'd sensed something odd in the fact that a friend who'd died six years ago had appeared in London...or if she'd registered Hel's true feelings about Natsunagi... In either case, she might have found her way to the correct conclusion a year ago."

...I see. So Siesta had been just like me and Natsunagi.

We'd all lost precious memories and made some misunderstanding, but now we were filling in the missing pieces one by one.

"So even Siesta gets things wrong," I said, although it really didn't need saying.

"Yes, she's human." SIESTA's response was casual. "...Unlike me," she added, a little lonely.

"Listen, SIESTA, you're..."

Just as I started to speak, it happened.

"Your phone's ringing," SIESTA pointed out, and I noticed that the smartphone I'd set on the table was vibrating. The screen read *Fuubi Kase*. Phone calls from her almost never meant good news; I had a bad feeling about this one as I pressed the TALK button.

"I've got bad news and bad news. Which do you want first?"

"That's not even a choice..." I hung my head. Just what I was afraid of.

On the other end of the line, I heard a long sigh, and I could imagine the smoke.

"Ms. Fuubi, when are you actually going to quit smoking?"

She'd declared she was quitting at least twice already. I'd been right there both times.

"Well, I always want to quit. The damn things just won't leave my lips alone."

"Why don't you find yourself a guy instead?"

"I'll hang up on you."

...Uh, you're the one who called.

"So? What is this bad news?"

I'd have preferred not to hear it, but since she'd called me, it probably involved me. In that case, it was better to find out fast.

"Right. First off." Ms. Fuubi paused for a beat, then dropped a bomb: "—Seed and Bat have teamed up."

"So you really do know about Seed, Ms. Fuubi."

In the past I'd forgotten, Ms. Fuubi had retrieved me from the island after Siesta's death. Apparently her ties to SPES ran deeper than I'd thought.

"Yeah, I figured you'd be finding out soon." As if doing me one better, Ms. Fuubi languidly exhaled her cigarette smoke. "Anyways, I dunno what the deal is, but apparently Seed helped Bat pull off a jailbreak. You kids keep a sharp eye out, too."

"Bat broke out of jail, and he's with Seed..." But Bat had rebelled against SPES four years ago. As punishment, he'd been ordered to pull off that skyjack at ten thousand meters. Why would he team up with the leader of SPES now?

"And then, the other bad news is..."

Just as she was about to tell me the rest, my doorbell rang.

"Visitor?" Ms. Fuubi's tone was suddenly grim.

At this point, I didn't even have to ask what she was worried about, but... "I'm going to answer that."

"Hey, I'm trying to tell you—"

"I know. I've got some insurance, though."

In the unlikely event that the visitor was him, SIESTA was here. She and I exchanged glances, and I headed for the entryway.

"Besides, he's got no reason to come after me now."

Grumbling—and certain that Bat was standing right outside—I turned the knob. "Still, he's got pretty good manners if he's ringing the door... bell?"

When I opened the door and saw who was actually there, I was incredibly confused. "S-Saikawa?"

Those pink hair streaks, and the eye patch over her left eye. By now, there was no way I could have mistaken her for anyone else. My visitor was the impudent Yui Saikawa, the world's cutest idol.

"Kimizuka, please be my producer!"

She was looking up at me. As usual, she completely failed to read the room.

6 years ago, Yui

"No matter what happens, don't ever let anyone separate you from that left eye."

They'd done the surgery while I was sleeping. By the time I woke up, it was all over.

I was lying in bed, and Mom was talking to me. "People may try to take it from you, but don't listen to them. You have to protect it."

Her voice and face were stricter than I'd ever heard or seen them, but the hand she held out was gentle. Softly, she touched the bandages over my left eye.

"Do you mean I'm soooo cute that all the world's kidnappers are after me?"

"You may be my daughter, but you're so tough no one would ever believe you'd just come out of surgery." Mom laid a hand on my forehead and sighed.

What on earth was this about?

"Dear, say something to her." She turned to my dad.

"Just look how adorable my daughter is."

"She grew up this way because of you, you know." Mom's head drooped again.

Yup, my dad spoils me rotten. If I say I want bread, he goes out and buys me an entire cake, and if I say I want a bicycle, he gives me a cruise ship. Thanks to that, I already know how to pilot a boat.

Well, it's a trade-off. I still can't ride a bike.

"But, Yui, you do know *things can't go on like this*, don't you?" Mom turned to me again. She didn't look angry—just sort of sad and uneasy. "Someday, you'll have to go outside."

I may have been young, but I knew that when Mom said "outside," she didn't mean it literally. It was a word she always used when she was trying to convince me.

"You'll need to make friends."

I didn't have a single friend. I hadn't even spent much time in school.

"...It's fine. Talking with lots of people isn't any fun."

Kids always exclude anybody that isn't like them.

I was born blind in my left eye, so that was one thing that made me different. The fact that my family was rich might have been part of the problem too.

There was always an invisible line between me and the rest of the group, and I wasn't allowed to cross it. A wall of air barred my way.

"As long as you and Dad are here, I don't need anything else." I'd told her so before, and I said it again today. Then I pulled the covers up over my head.

"We won't be able to protect you forever, you know." Mom gave another big sigh; she sounded sort of tired. I'm smart, though; I know how to handle her at times like this.

"...You're going away?" I peeked out from under the futon, speaking in a little baby voice.

"D-don't turn those puppy eyes on me, Yui." Mom hugged me tightly.

Yeah, my mom is actually the one who spoils me the most. Still, it's hard to believe I could trick her this easily. I might have a knack for the idol life.

"Yui," Dad said. Setting a hand on Mom's shoulder, he separated us gently. "Let's take that bandage off, all right?"

I'd secretly been avoiding this, but he was sharp, and he'd seen right through me.

"...Okay."

I was a little tense, but his serious gaze pushed me to take the plunge. I reached up for the white fabric that was wrapped around my head, over my left eye, and slipped it off.

"All right. Take a look."

I peeked into the hand mirror my dad held out to me. "It's so pretty..."

The blue eye shone like a sapphire, and I caught myself sighing over it. My parents had gotten this false eye for me.

"That eye suits you better than anyone else, Yui. We want you to wear lovely dresses and light up the world. You'll shine like this jewel." As my father spoke, he looked more serious than I'd ever seen him. "That eye will light your way and help you find what matters most to you. And so..." He gazed at me. "No matter what, you must never let anyone separate you from it."

He said the same thing Mom had.

"...Dear, don't steal the scene like that," Mom complained.

"If I didn't, I wouldn't get to be the cool dad at all." He nodded away, straight-faced.

My parents get along so well.

Someday, it would be great if I found people I could have this much fun talking with...

I'm kidding. That was a joke. These two are all I need.

And so—

"No, you still weren't very cool."

""Aww...""

...I provided the punchline for them.

Still... Even so, someday...

If I take a flying leap into the outside world...if I find friends who'll accept me as I am, and I don't have to hide things or keep secrets...will life be more fun?

Heh-heh. For some reason, seeing this blue eye made me feel like giving it a whirl.

I'll go big this time.

I only thought of it a minute ago, but maybe I will work toward becoming an idol singer.

Chapter 2

◆ Hmm. So you're my producer, are you?

"I smell another woman."

Out of the frying pan, into the fire. We'd solved one case, but that didn't mean all the trouble was over. Right after Natsunagi and Hel had resolved their business, Yui Saikawa the super idol had turned up on my doorstep with a new problem.

This sort of thing had happened before, hadn't it? Not only that, but due to a certain situation, she'd appointed me her producer.

"Saikawa, don't go around sniffing my apartment."

Saikawa was making snuffling noises like a puppy, and I gave her a disapproving look. We'd just been talking about a serious issue, and now this? Maybe I shouldn't have let her in?

"Hm. I'm picking up a suspicious scent from this direction."

"I told you, knock it off."

Saikawa was just about to open the door to my bedroom, and I gave her a little shove.

"Ow! Kimizuka, you're the only person anywhere who'd hit the world's most adorable super idol." Tears beaded in her eyes as she pressed a hand to her head.

"Adorably irritating" is a more accurate descriptor than "adorable," I thought as I told her off. "That's my bedroom. No trespassing."

"It's fine. I took a shower before I came."

"I don't get why that would make it okay."

Besides, more importantly... "Natsunagi's sleeping in there. Don't disturb her."

Sharing her memories with Hel had been a stressful experience, and she still hadn't woken up.

"Oh-ho? Kimizuka, have you finally become a man?"

"What is wrong with you? It's a complicated situation, all right?" I wanted to fill her in on stuff, that situation included, so I wished she'd hurry up and get back to her seat.

"I'm sorry to keep you waiting."

Just then, SIESTA emerged from the kitchen, carrying a tray with tea for three on it. Even though I knew she wasn't the real one, the sight of Siesta in a maid outfit serving us from my kitchen was certainly a thing.

"Unpleasant gaze detected. I will eliminate the source immediately."

"Don't go full android on me. Put that gun down right now."

"Hmm. Your couples' comedy routine is alive and well, I see. You're making me a little jealous over here."

"It's not a competition, Saikawa. Let's get back on topic." As we drank our tea, I shifted the conversation back to what we'd originally been talking about. "So, is it true? Your parents are *suspected of fraudulent accounting*?"

That was what Saikawa had told me ten minutes earlier, when she'd stopped by out of the blue.

Saikawa's wealthy parents were suspected of having conducted some sort of illegal accounting. It was just now coming to light.

"...Yes. Well, I don't know the whole truth yet, but the news will probably be on TV and online tomorrow. The media are already swarming my house." Saikawa took a sip of her tea. She looked a little discouraged.

"I see... And so you escaped over here in the middle of the night?"

That had been Ms. Fuubi's second piece of bad news.

Bat's jailbreak, and the scandal involving Saikawa's parents: Both were problems I couldn't afford to ignore.

"Yes. I'm looking for a place that will shelter me for a little while."

I see. So this was a *request from a client*. But... "Wouldn't it be better to ask Natsunagi about that?" If she was going to be a freeloader, staying with Natsunagi would be a more convenient option than staying with a guy. Besides, at this point, she'd gladly lend Saikawa a hand as a detective.

"Yes, you're right. And so what I want you to do, Kimizuka, is be my producer," she said, finally getting back to the initial subject. "It's going to be hard to go home or visit my agency for a while. I thought it might be faster to have you take over as producer."

"Saikawa, are you trying to fob off an insane odd job on me?" I mean, I wasn't trying to belittle the production industry by calling it an odd job, but come on.

"Congratulations, Kimizuka. Starting today, you are both the ace detective's assistant and an idol singer's producer."

"Yeah, I sure feel like a winner..." I slumped back in my chair, sighing. "I guess I could do it, though."

"...Huh? You will? You stopped fighting that really fast."

Yeah, because pacing is important with stuff like this. That was something Siesta had told me to "work on improving" multiple times way back when.

"If I'm going to be your producer, then I'll have to stick close to you, right? The security at this place isn't good enough to really protect you, though."

After all, this building was thirty years old. It didn't have automatic locks, and the toilets didn't even come with the standard bidet function. My apartment was a cheap one-bedroom; the rent was only 36,000 yen.

"In that case, you're welcome to use my house," SIESTA offered. "It has a decent number of rooms, plus a stock of groceries and daily necessities. The security is stricter than a downtown high-rise apartment building. It's entirely underground, and I lived there in secret for close to a year without being detected."

"I see. The room where you had us locked up, huh?"

In terms of space and safety, that place did sound as if it would fit the bill. Besides, there was one other thing I needed to be concerned about right now: Bat.

Natsunagi and I were his enemies. Now that he'd broken out of jail, we should probably lie low until we knew what he was planning... I'd also just been thinking it would be nice to get a break from my summer classes, so this was perfect.

"I see. So we'll be *cohabiting*?" Saikawa murmured, putting a fingertip to her chin.

Cohabiting—Siesta had joked about that with me lots of times. For three whole years, it had been just the two of us on that dizzying journey with no clear destination. It was true that we'd spent several nights under one roof. She always got such a kick out of that. She'd smiled at me and called it "cohabiting." But I'd always responded the same way.

"We're just strategic roommates."

"I heard everything!" Just then, with a click, the door behind us opened.

"...Natsunagi, don't interrupt me when I'm sounding cool."

We'd been right in the middle of the scene where my melancholy, sentimental profile stole the spotlight.

"I heard 'cohabitation,' and it just happened. It's a fun word." Natsunagi joined us at the kitchen table.

...*Geez, she's always like this.* She didn't seem tense at all. "Is everything okay now?" I asked casually. I meant her health and the past she'd just learned about, plus her resolution to become the ace detective.

"Yeah. It's okay."

It was just a brief exchange. However, from Natsunagi's clear, determined profile, I could tell she wasn't lying.

She'd shouldered Siesta's will...and probably Alicia's as well.

In front of that mirror, she'd settled accounts with her past.

"Now then, to recap—for now, we'll shelter Saikawa and move into Siesta's hideout. Any objections?" Attempting to wrap up the discussion, I checked with Siesta, Natsunagi, and Saikawa.

"Except for the fact that you're taking charge of a discussion regarding the use of my house, I have no complaints."

"As long as I ignore the fact that you're acting like the protagonist even though I'm the detective, no objections here."

"If I said I wasn't afraid to live under the same roof as Kimizuka, I'd be lying, but I'll put up with it!"

"...Great. So we're all agreed."

And that's how the four of us began strategically rooming together.

"No, I have—!!!"

A sullen-looking blond agent burst in immediately afterward, but that's another story.

◆ Use proper Japanese

The next morning.

"—! I'm terribly sorry... I would— Yes, I'd like to refrain from giving an official response regarding that matter... Yes, if you'll excuse me."

The producer's lackluster apology echoed in an underground room.

The only thing I could really do was keep telling the unseen people on the other end of the line that I was sorry. I didn't know if there was actually any point to this; I was acting on my employer's orders... Seems like I've always been somebody's employee.

So, yesterday evening, I'd moved to Siesta's hideout. Early in the morning, after a nap, I'd started doing the work Saikawa had assigned to me. Every few minutes, somebody called the cell phone she'd given me with questions about the scandal or messages about jobs.

As an aside, Siesta, the master of this house, had been gone since last night. She'd said she was concerned about Bat's movements. I'd offered to help her, but she'd told me to "just concentrate on being Yui Saikawa's producer," and so here I was.

"'Labor is evil,' huh..." Finally managing to hang up, I sighed, gazing at the cell phone.

There was no way I could have successfully learned how to be an idol singer's producer in a day. Without the magic words "my supervisor is currently absent," I would've snapped under the stress and smashed the phone on the floor by now.

"...Man, this is ugly." I shot a sidelong glance at the variety show on the living room TV.

As Saikawa had predicted yesterday, they were discussing her parents' scandal. A commentator who wasn't any sort of expert was throwing out all sorts of wild guesses and insisting that Saikawa herself had an obligation to explain.

"Oh, shut up, dude. Don't you talk about Saikawa." My irritation got the better of me; I yanked the cord out of the wall, and the TV went dark.

"...Haaah. I guess I'd better go wake them up."

When I looked at the clock, it was almost noon, but there was still no sign of the other three. For starters, I headed for the room where Natsunagi and Saikawa were sleeping.

"Heeey, it's almost...noon...?"

The first thing I saw when I stepped inside was two girls lying in bed. The covers had slipped off just a bit to reveal Natsunagi hugging Saikawa to her like a stuffed animal. Both girls were in their pajamas. They were breathing peacefully, and their tranquil faces were so sacred I wanted to gaze at them forever—but that wasn't why I was here.

"C'mon. I'll make breakfast for you, so get up already."

They were both out cold, but I shook them awake.

"Mm... Breeeakfast? I want Schau Essen sausageees..." Natsunagi finally made it back from dreamland, rubbing her eyes.

"We don't have Schau Essen, but we've got regular wieners, so hurry and wake up."

"Yaaawn... Mm, I want to eat thaaat... Kimizuka's wieneeer..."

"Natsunagi, go wash your face already. I'll pretend I didn't hear that."

"Nooo, no, Natsunagiii... Kimizuka's Kimizuka is more a fiiish sausage than a wieneeer..."

"Saikawa, you can't say stuff like that just because you're half asleep, all right? Wait, this means you even make fun of me subconsciously."

I yanked the covers off them, then turned the thermostat down to eighteen degrees Celsius and left the room.

Charlie was next.

Since there were only two bedrooms, we'd played rock-paper-scissors to decide who'd sleep where last night. Unfortunately, I'd ended up sharing with Charlie. She slept way rougher than I'd thought, and she'd kept waking me up. But now *she* was trying to sleep.

As I was plotting the best way to get my revenge, I opened the bedroom door and saw—

"Charlie, what the heck are you doing?"

Charlie had her face buried in a pillow and was sniffing it loudly.

"That's the pillow I was using..."

"K-Kimizuka?! Oh— Th-this isn't what it looks like! You've got it all wrong!"

"...Uh. Well, you know. Different people have different, uh, preferences, so, yeah..."

"Hey, don't take this so seriously! At least get mad! Hey! Look at me! Stop acting so uncomfortable!" Sweating bullets, Charlie desperately struggled to explain herself. "That wasn't it! I thought I caught Ma'am's scent on this pillow! That's the only reason I was smelling it!"

"...I think that might also be a problem."

"—! That does it! I'll have to steal your memories!" With a wild gleam in her eyes, Charlie tried to shove me down onto the bed. "Sorry to do this when you just got your memories back, but I'm taking eighteen years' worth of knowledge and experience!"

"That's too much! Are you planning to turn me into an adult-size baby?"

"Don't worry. I don't know about Nagisa, but that'll probably suit Yui's tastes nicely."

"Hey, what sort of tastes are you assigning your friends?"

Charlie roughly pushed me down onto the bed. "Just give up." She leaned over me, her face red with anger and agitation, and just then—

"What are you two doing?"

The door stood open. Saikawa was watching us coldly. "Are you one of those 'frenemy couples'?"

""No!""

We accidentally spoke in unison. We couldn't afford to match up on anything else.

"Saikawa, that's not it. You've got it all wrong!"

Then, as I was trying to fumble my way through an excuse...

"—Double. Kill."

Natsunagi looked down on us with eyes so frigid it made the air-conditioning seem lukewarm. Then she walked out, slamming the door behind her.

"Th-this isn't that, Nagisa! It was an assident!"

"You mean 'accident'!!!"

◆ Later on, the assistant ate and enjoyed it

After the "rise and shine" mess was over...

"I see it now."

Natsunagi was standing in the kitchen wearing an apron. She was holding a ladle like a professional baseball player predicting her home run, and her eyes were narrowed keenly. When I'd started getting ready to make breakfast after that earlier trouble, she'd insisted on taking over for me.

She hadn't been the only one.

"Can you even cook, Nagisa?" Charlie goaded her, also wearing an apron.

"Charlie...I'd never lose to you!"

"Huh. Then should we settle our score here and now?"

The two of them glared daggers at each other in front of the sink.

"Those two never seem to get along, do they?" Behind them, Saikawa murmured. She had her elbows propped on the table, with her chin resting in her hands. Natsunagi and Charlie had met about a week ago on that cruise and quarreled over Siesta.

"Having a cooking showdown as a proxy battle seems like a weird idea, but..."

I was at the table with Saikawa, watching the other two with a distant look in my eyes. They'd appointed us as judges for their contest... If their relationship had progressed to the fighting stage, though, this couldn't be all bad. It seemed a lot healthier than feeling awkward about things that had happened a year ago, anyway.

"Well, I can't imagine I'd lose to a girl like you, Nagisa." Charlie combed her fingers through the blond hair she was so proud of.

"—! I'm the one who's going to capture Kimizuka's heart through his stomach!" Natsunagi retorted impulsively, but...

"...? Huh? What kind of contest was this again?"

"I was joking," she muttered quickly, then turned to face forward.

"Kimizuka, can we get a quote about how incredibly cute Nagisa just was?"

"I didn't hear it. I couldn't hear a thing." Instead, I turned to Natsunagi. "By the way, what are you making?"

"A sauté of blue Breton lobster and seasonal vegetables with mousseline sauce, maybe?"

"Are you planning to turn this into a cooking battle manga?"

Ignoring me, Natsunagi got a red lobster out of the fridge. *Wait, she's actually got the ingredients for that? Siesta eats way too well.*

"…Um, so. Get good and hungry while you wait."

Turning back around, Natsunagi winked and pointed the ladle at me.

"That's weird."

More than half an hour later, Natsunagi was floundering in the kitchen. She was watching the microwave. Inside it, *something that used to be food* was writhing like a black monster, apparently trying to burst out through the door. It was a disaster.

"But as long as I don't open this door, we can't say for sure that I messed it up, can we?"

"This isn't Schrödinger's cat. You've gotta open it sometime."

Is she planning to make it so we can never use the microwave again?

"Ngh, I always make my own lunches, even…" Natsunagi's shoulders slumped with dejection.

"Honestly! If you hadn't tried to get so fancy out of nowhere, this wouldn't have happened." Charlie gave a disgusted snort at the mess. "I'll make you some regular fried rice, so just sit tight."

She pointed the frying pan at us as if it were a gun, then twirled back to the stove.

"That's weird." Charlie stood in front of the stove, racking her brains.

It had been another thirty minutes, and—I can't say I was surprised— there was a mound of scorched black stuff in the frying pan.

"Maybe it's one of those things that looks unfortunate but tastes surprisingly good?"

"If you really think that, eat it yourself. Don't keep glancing at me."

Sorry, but I'm completely sick of those two-panel, instant punchline comics.

"…I'm always busy, so I can't cook for myself."

Maybe living that way was part of being an agent. Charlie fidgeted with her hair, making excuses.

"Geez. This is going nowhere."

Just then, our savior arrived.

"It's lunchtime already. I'll do it!" Rising from her judge's chair, Saikawa tied on an apron and headed for the kitchen. "I'd like to have something ready to eat on hand too, so I'll make curry. Nagisa, you cut up the meat. Charlie, steam another batch of rice, please." Saikawa began dicing vegetables with a practiced hand.

"O-okay..."

"Um, sure..."

Shoulders hunched in embarrassment, Natsunagi and Charlie accepted Saikawa's orders.

"Why is it that Saikawa always ends up being the most reliable one?" She was the only middle schooler in this group, too...

Saikawa overheard my mutter. "Heh-heh! I've been through quite a lot, you know." She glanced at me over her shoulder, smiling wryly, and kept right on cutting vegetables as she did it.

Saikawa had lost her parents three years ago. I wondered suddenly if that was when she'd started cooking for herself.

"So I'm two steps ahead of both of you—younger and better at housekeeping."

However, that glimpse of what she'd been through only lasted a moment before Saikawa began taunting the older girls... I don't even have to tell you what the results were.

"Yui?"

"Uh, Yui?"

She was between two pairs of eyes glaring daggers that could have killed a wild animal.

"...K-Kimizuka. They're scaring me..."

"Yeah, that's one hundred percent your fault."

◆ It's your story

The morning had been one thing after another, so I figured the rest of the day would be relatively peaceful, but I was dead wrong.

Saikawa's work phone was ringing constantly, and it was all I could do to keep up. Meanwhile, Natsunagi, Saikawa, and Charlie had fun chatting and playing board games... *C'mon, you people do some work too.*

In any case, I'd spent the whole day working, but now I was finally taking a nice, long bath.

"...I'm beat."

My voice echoed in the empty bathroom. Being alone made me remember that way too much had been happening lately. There was the kidnapping Siesta had set up, where we'd learned the truth of her death. Then, with Siesta's help, Natsunagi had remembered more of her past and even reconciled with her other personality. After that, just as one problem had been solved, here came Bat's jailbreak and Saikawa's scandal. Saikawa, Natsunagi, Charlie, and I had been forced to move to Siesta's hideout. We were living the fugitive life now.

"Yeesh. Not fair." As I sighed, the same old ugly phrase slipped out. But this was a huge situation, and it had only been a few days. Nobody could blame me for complaining a little.

"...Siesta."

And nobody could blame me for calling my old partner's name, either. Yeah, it's not as if I missed her or anythi...

"Man, this is bad."

When did I get so weak?

I knew the answer to that right away. One year ago—on that day— Siesta had died, and now here I was. I shut my eyes to the truth, forgot my mission, fled into routine, and solved the little incidents I got dragged into. That was all I'd done, but I'd lied to myself and said I was carrying out the detective's last wish.

What about me had changed since then?

I'd met Natsunagi, learned what Siesta felt, remembered my mission through Saikawa's incident, and truly inherited the detective's will after Charlie scolded me.

Had I had the wrong idea about all of that, though?

I hadn't known Siesta's past or Natsunagi's. In the end, I was no different than I had been on that day. I was obliviously soaking in that same tepid water, just the way I'd—

"Guess I'll get out."

While I wasn't paying attention, the bath had gone stone cold.

If I'd stayed in this water long enough, I bet I'd eventually have frozen to death, I thought. My head had cooled.

"Whoa. I may have to take back that 'fish sausage' remark."

Suddenly I realized that the bathroom door was open, and Saikawa was standing right in front of me.

...Saikawa was standing right in front of me?

"Geez! What are you doing?!" I hastily ducked back down into the bath.

"Well, you know. I've been causing a lot of trouble, so I thought I'd at least wash your back."

"You're causing trouble for me right this minute! Shut the door, now!"

"Oh, honestly. If I must." Sounding resigned, Saikawa closed the bathroom door. "There we go."

"...Why are you still in here?"

"Huh? Taking a bath while chatting with a young girl was your greatest and only pleasure, wasn't it?"

"Saikawa, is trashing my reputation a hobby of yours? ...Besides, she was just really funny, that's all." Come to think of it, something like that had happened with Siesta, way back when.

"By the way, Kimizuka—you can shoo me out into the dressing room, but my left eye can see you naked through the door."

"Turn around, right now. You're only allowed to see me naked if you're prepared to let me see you naked."

"You're acting like that's a witty comment, but you really just want to take a bath with a girl, right?"

Man, Saikawa's comebacks are top of the line.

"Huh, I see... So you and Siesta did this, too. That's informative."

"Don't literally take notes. That's not going to be on any high school entrance exam," I told Saikawa through the bathroom door. "And, uh, I'd like to get out now."

Then I chased Saikawa out of the dressing room and left the bathroom.

"The thing is, I've realized I don't know much about Siesta." Saikawa apparently wasn't done with our conversation. This time, she talked to me through the dressing room door while I dried off. "Did you notice, Kimizuka? Siesta and I have no real connection to each other." Now that she mentioned it, that was true. "Natsunagi and Charlie's ties to her are much firmer. Natsunagi has inherited Siesta's heart, and Charlie is Siesta's first apprentice."

"Only according to Charlie, but yeah."

Still, I got what she was trying to say. Both Natsunagi and Charlie had met Siesta personally, a long time ago. Saikawa, though—

"Oh, but don't think I'm trying to say I feel left out." On the other side of the door, Saikawa sounded flustered. "You see, I think it's why I'm able to stay neutral, to a certain extent."

"Neutral?"

"Yes. For example, say the circumstances that surround us are a story. Who do you suppose is at the center of it?"

That was a pretty abstract question. Even so, one person instantly came to mind.

"That would be Siesta."

I'd finished dressing, and I opened the door...but Saikawa wasn't there.

"Yes, I think so too."

I heard her voice from the living room. Did she mean we were supposed to continue this conversation in there?

"Well, without her, this story wouldn't even have started."

I'd been Siesta's assistant for three years. Natsunagi was Siesta's old friend, her mortal enemy—and now the inheritor of her heart. Charlie had looked up to Siesta as a teacher, and she still did. We were currently dealing with SPES, the enemy Siesta had been ordered to defeat.

The story that surrounded us was focused entirely on Siesta. She was the axis around which the world turned.

"But while I'm part of all that, I'm distant from Siesta. I'm the only one who is."

When I went back to the dining room, Saikawa was there. She was holding a mug in both hands and blowing on it. "It's hot milk. Have some, Kimizuka."

"It's summer," I told her, but she already had some waiting for me, which made arguing sort of pointless. I sat down across from her.

"That being the case, there may be something I in particular am allowed to say. Isn't that right, Kimizuka?"

I took another look at Saikawa. I'd been in such a hurry earlier that I hadn't really seen her.

She was wearing pink pajamas, and I could smell the sweet smell of someone who'd just gotten out of the bath. Her hair hung loose. She wasn't wearing her eye patch, and her left eye was as beautiful as a blue jewel.

"This is our story."

She smiled. "It's Natsunagi's story, and Charlie's, and yours, Kimizuka. It belongs to each of you. So all that matters is the question of what you want to do. I think that's enough," she said. She took a long, luxurious sip of her hot milk.

"Huh? Actually, no matter how you look at it, I'm the central figure in this incident. Why am I the one who's helping you, instead of the other way around? Kimizuka, show a little more enthusiasm and lend me a hand, all right?"

"That was the most unfair thing this century."

◆ Produce an idol: A simple, pain-in-the-butt job

The next day...

Saikawa and I left Siesta's residence in the morning by car. It was Yui Saikawa's private car, and her private chauffeur was behind the wheel.

"Still, we're leaving really early. The program's not till this evening, right?" I asked. Saikawa was sitting in the back seat next to me, gazing at her phone.

Today, she was scheduled to perform in a live music program. We'd gone into hiding to protect Saikawa from the media, but they hadn't been able to cancel that live broadcast. Now I was going with her.

"I have a lot I need to do beforehand. After all, I am a super idol."
Saikawa put her phone away, then gave a big, feline yawn.

"You look really tired. Didn't get much sleep yesterday?"

"No. After you and I spoke, we girls talked far into the night." Saikawa
let her head fall onto my shoulder and closed her eyes. *Man, this idol's public and private faces are so different... Actually, I can't believe how much she
relaxes around me.*

"By the way, what were you girls talking about?"

"Mm, how much you suck, mostly."

"I shouldn't have asked." Well, if they'd bonded with each other by tear-
ing me down, that was fine... Maybe?

"They couldn't come with us today, though?" Saikawa sat up. I wasn't
sure whether she was uneasy about having me be her only escort, or
whether she was just curious.

"Yeah. We have Bat to worry about too."

With Seed's help, Bat had broken out of jail. We didn't know what he
wanted, but there was a decent possibility that he'd go after Siesta's will
on Seed's orders—and after Natsunagi, who was succeeding her as ace
detective. Based on that assumption, I'd decided to keep Natsunagi in the
safest place possible and have Charlie guard her.

"Um, Mr. Bat, wasn't it? Isn't Siesta dealing with him now?"

"Yeah, she should be, but..." As a matter of fact, I'd gotten a text from
Siesta early that morning. I read it to Saikawa.

"'Leave this to me. Kimihiko, you just watch over Yui Saikawa's decision.' End quote."

I didn't really understand what she was trying to say.

Not "protect" her—"watch over" her.

Did it mean she didn't expect anything from me in a fight? I mean, yeah,
I hadn't been able to do much over those three years, just watch over
Siesta from the shadows, but...

"I see. Siesta knows you very well, doesn't she?" Somewhere in there,
Saikawa had gotten out her phone and was gazing at it again. "Watch
over me. That's perfect for a concert-lurker-wannabe-boyfriend-geek like
you, Kimizuka."

"Saikawa, you think I'll forgive you no matter what you say to me, don't
you?"

"Yes, I do."

Oh. She does? She doesn't even sound sorry.

"After all, no matter what happens, I believe you'll always be on my
side."

"You definitely put your foot in your mouth; don't try to flip it around
and act like that was a positive exchange."

"Hey, it looks like we're just about there." She forcibly derailed the conversation. That's a move I use a lot too, though, so I couldn't really call her
on it.

"Hm... We're headed to the TV station, right?"

I'd been distracted and hadn't noticed until now, but when I glanced out
the window, I realized we'd left the city. As the car drove on, the clusters
of buildings disappeared, and all I could see were old-fashioned houses
and timeworn signs.

"Kimizuka, we're here."

The car stopped, and on Saikawa's instructions, I got out.

"Where's 'here'?"

I shaded my eyes against the bright summer sun.

Blue sky and a green ridgeline. There were cicadas crying in the trees
right next to us, and the place smelled like summer. This land might as
well have been untouched by civilization, there to make you forget all
about the big city.

"All right. Let's go, then."

Apparently, we still had to walk a bit. Sunlight lanced through the white
clouds as Saikawa marched down a country road, leading the way.

"It looks like we're heading for a hill. Is there something at the top?"

"What? Oh, yes, a hot spring!"

...I totally wasn't expecting that.

"Heh-heh! An idol and her producer on a forbidden romantic escape!"

"...You'd better not be serious."

"No good? Eloping to a hidden rural bath... Oh, I like the way that
sounded. I'll put it in the lyrics for my next single." Ignoring me, Saikawa

got out a notepad. I felt the birth of a famous—or rather, infamous—song coming on. But more importantly...

"Saikawa. Are you afraid of the media?"

I thought I saw her shoulders flinch.

"What are you talking about, Kimizuka?" She kept walking without turning around.

Saikawa didn't complain easily. She kept her idol smile pasted on her face, and she always hid her true feelings behind it.

"I mean, if I'm wrong, that's fine."

We continued down the path, through lush greenery and the stifling scent of sunbaked grass.

◆ Scream at the unfairness of the world

"Here we are. This is it."

I'd picked up on the fact that she'd been lying about the hot spring, but I definitely hadn't expected this destination.

"This is where my mom and dad are." Gently, Saikawa knelt in front of the gravestone that stood at the top of the hill. "Actually, this whole area belongs to the Saikawa family. I had them buried here because the view is so good." As Saikawa spoke, she lit a stick of incense.

"Can I pay my respects, too?"

"Yes, thank you. I'm sure they'd both love that."

I stood beside her, put my hands together, and closed my eyes.

I'd never met Saikawa's parents, of course. However, I did know how she felt, and I offered a silent prayer.

"Thank you very much." A soft breeze blew, and Saikawa raised her head and smiled. "I think they're both relieved that I've found a life partner."

"You've gotta be kidding me. It's already okay to joke around again?"

"Yes. My parents liked never-ending comedy routines even more than I do."

"You inherited this from your parents. Unbelievable."

We cracked up a little.

"...Somehow, though, I still feel like I'm dreaming."

"Dreaming?"

"Yes. How should I put it...? It's like it's all one spectacular practical joke. Sometimes I think they're both actually alive, and pretty soon they'll jump out from behind something and give me a good scare."

As she spoke, her profile looked lonelier than I'd ever seen it. It might have been three years, but for Saikawa, the reality of her parents' death hadn't faded... Just like one year hadn't been enough for me.

"In the end, being on my own makes me uneasy. I always want to have someone watching me."

"Is that why you're an idol?"

"...Yes, that could be part of it," Saikawa responded absently. She was hugging her knees. "Besides, long ago, my dad told me he hoped I'd live my life wearing pretty dresses. He said he wanted me to light up the world. Mom was constantly telling me to run outside into the world and make friends. And so I—" Saikawa appeared to be fondly remembering the past. "I may not be able to stay an idol forever, though. After all, a global crisis may be just around the corner."

"Really? I think an idol who sings, dances, and sometimes fights pseudo-humans would be pretty entertaining."

Just as there used to be an ace detective who knew a whole bunch about idols from Japón.

"...Heh-heh. Your persuasion tactics are as funny as ever, Kimizuka." Saikawa smiled, smoothly rising to her feet.

"But sometimes—I get a little tired."

She murmured the words in a small voice, without looking at me. Then, surveying the scenery that spread out below us, she stretched luxuriously. "Nnnnnnn...! It really is nice to be out in nature, isn't it!" Saikawa was still facing away from me, but her voice was as cheerful as could be. "What do you think? Should we pitch my job and everything else out the window and actually start a new life in the country together?"

"I don't think a sheltered rich girl from the city could manage that."

"Oh, that's not true. I can cook, and living off the land will be easy-peasy."

"Maybe for a few days, but you'd be missing convenience stores and Wi-Fi before too long."

"...You're no fun." My reaction seemed to displease Saikawa; she took out her phone and started to fiddle with it. Definitely snubbing me. "Witty retorts are fine, but if you're negative about everything, people won't like you."

"I see. You've got me there," I responded lightly, although I'd quietly gotten to my feet and was sneaking up behind Saikawa. "—But I don't mind being disliked for now." I snatched her smartphone out of her hands.

"Wha—! G-give that back!" Saikawa jumped, trying to grab the phone as I held it high in the air. However, it's not that easy to make up a height difference of twenty-plus centimeters. "Why are you picking on me?! Is it because I was playing with my phone while I talked about wanting to live in the country?! In that case—"

"No."

...*Yeesh. Let me be a little nosy, at least.* Keeping Saikawa at bay, I showed her the phone's screen. "It's because you've been staring at this stuff all day."

The screen showed the timeline of a certain social networking site. It was filled with nasty comments about Saikawa after that news report.

Saikawa never showed weakness. Before she was an idol singer, though, she was a girl in her last year of middle school. The news over the past few days had to be getting to her.

"...Give that back, please."

"Mm. Sorry."

Saikawa took the phone from me, then lowered her head guiltily. "I don't care what they say about me." She bit her lip, turning off her phone. "But when they go after Mom and Dad...I just can't take it."

Saikawa's parents were her guiding star. She couldn't allow them to be tainted... That said, she didn't have any significant way to turn the situation around right now. Her enemy was an enormous, shapeless cruelty. There had never been a way to fight that.

—Even so, if there was one thing we could do now, it was...

"Kimizuka?"

I'd taken a few steps forward. Saikawa gazed at me, mystified.

...*Sorry, Saikawa. This is about all I can come up with.*

I sucked in a deep breath, and—

"Dammit, you can't do this to meeeeeeee!"

On the top of the hill, I screamed my guts out at the landscape below.

"K-Kimizuka?"

Saikawa's gloomy expression had turned to shock. "Um, I mean, I'm very happy that you're getting angry on my behalf, but it's rather embarrassing..."

"You can't just go off and die a hero all by yourself! You're so *stupid*, Siestaaaaaaaa!"

"O-oh, was that what this was...!" Saikawa's retort sounded unusually flustered.

Sorry. I accidentally let the scream of my soul slip out there.

But...

"Okay, Saikawa." I turned to her, holding out a hand. "Go ahead and vent. Let it all out."

If it wasn't possible to change someone, or something, then it had to at least be okay to scream all the unfairness out.

"...Are idols allowed to use dirty words?"

"You aren't on the clock yet anyway."

Until that live broadcast started, Yui Saikawa was just a girl in her third year of middle school.

She was allowed to say whatever she wanted.

Here and now, at least.

"—————! Bastaaaaaards!"

Beside me, Saikawa shouted with her entire body.

Taking off her eye patch, she screamed at the reality that was hurting her, and at the unbearable unfairness of it all.

"You assholes don't know a thing!"

"You assholes—"

"Y-you!"

Then she sucked in a deep, deep breath, so big it seemed almost impossible, and—

"I love my mom and dad! Stop being mean to them and just shut uuuuuuuup!!!"

Her scream carried so far, I thought it might make it clear to heaven.

"...I wonder if they heard me."

Then Saikawa took a breath, getting herself under control. Her blue eye turned toward me. She looked as if she'd come back to her senses.

Of course, that wouldn't have resolved everything. At the very least, though, I had the feeling she'd sing her very best song after this.

"Yeah, that was a good scream. The radio towers could've picked that one up."

"Ah-ha-ha! It would be bad if my fans heard that, huh. But..." Saikawa looked up at me, clasping her hands behind her. "If they start flaming me, I'm counting on you to put out the fire. Okay, producer?"

The smile she gave me was as pure and open as a flower.

◆ Girls always want to wear pretty dresses

After that, we headed for the TV station again. Once Saikawa left me to go to her dressing room, I took advantage of my position as producer to duck into the studio.

This was the music program's special summer vacation edition, and it was being broadcast during the evening prime-time window. Lots of lights and cameras surrounded the set, and on the other side, the audience seats were filled with spectators.

"Performers on set."

When the program's start time came, a staff member called out, and the emcee, his assistant, and the featured artists walked in. The audience cheered. After several other performers, Saikawa entered, waving. In a sharp change from this morning, her makeup was flawless, and she was dressed in a frilly costume. That was Yui Saikawa the idol, all right. Her aura was in a whole different league.

But then something weird happened.

"...So that's really how it's going to go, huh?"

A slight stir ran through the audience. It was as if everyone had noticed something but was pretending they hadn't. That was true of the other performers as well. It didn't show on their faces, but somehow their smiles looked like an act.

I'd seen this coming, though. Saikawa was appearing on the show right in the middle of all that media coverage. It would have been weirder not to care about it. And yet when she realized the cameras were cutting her out, she smiled brightly and struck a pose. She was mugging for them.

Near me, a backstage staff member murmured, "Doesn't have much on her mind, does she?"

Seriously? Did he think Saikawa hadn't noticed the awkwardness? In that case, he'd flunk the Yui-nya Level 5 Certification exam.

"Times like this are when she smiles the most."

I folded my arms, watching over the broadcast from the back of the room.

During the program, the emcee talked with each artist, and then the artist performed their song. There were fifteen featured acts. About two hours into the program, Saikawa's turn came along.

"Next up is Miss Yui Saikawa."

As the emcee called her over, the camera zoomed in on Saikawa.

"Helloooo, it's Yui Saikawa! The world's cutest idol!" Striking another pose, Saikawa walked onto the set and stood next to the emcee. Then they talked about her latest single and her work for a minute or two.

So far, so good. But then...

"It sounds like you've had quite a mess on your hands lately," the emcee said, smiling thinly.

"...!" Saikawa's eyes flew open.

"Oh, come on! What was the point of that advance meeting, then?!" I bit my lip.

That morning, I'd discussed the flow for today's interview with the program's producer, and I'd specifically asked him—politely—not to bring up the scandal during the broadcast. Were they trying to generate a buzz, to boost their ratings? They'd brought up something everybody wanted answers on but couldn't ask about.

"Even if it was your parents who were directly responsible, I'd imagine it isn't possible to disassociate yourself from it," the man pressed. Saikawa had frozen up.

"You slimy little—" I almost stepped forward...but then my eyes met Saikawa's. She shook her head slightly, then turned back to the emcee.

"I'm sorry there's been such a commotion over my parents." She bowed her head meekly; she didn't try to sidestep the question. That set the studio buzzing. "However..." Saikawa looked up. "I am myself. Today, this is my show. And so for now, I'd love it if everyone focused on me."

She gave the emcee a goofy little smile.

"She's just trying to protect her image," somebody muttered.

Was it a performer, someone in the audience, a staff member, or a plant to make the show more exciting? Whichever it was, the voice that echoed quietly through the studio was trying to hurt Saikawa as much as they could.

"...You're right. I may be."

After a few seconds of silence, Saikawa nodded.

But I knew she wasn't the type of girl who'd let a thing like that end her. She'd gotten through her parents' death, she'd fought the enemies of the world, she'd shaken off the countless unfair things that had showered down on her, and here she was.

"Even so, I'm not going to stop. After all—" Once again, Saikawa smiled. She beamed.

"Idols always want to look pretty, you know."

Without looking at the emcee, Saikawa winked at the viewers on the other side of the camera.

The studio went very quiet.

In the back, a crew member rolled his arms in a signal.

"...And now it's time for Miss Yui Saikawa's performance." After a moment's hesitation, the emcee hastily got the show back on track.

However, *control* of the studio had already passed into the hands of one girl.

This was Saikawa's show, by Saikawa, for Saikawa's fans.

"Erm, the song is..."

Saikawa grabbed the mic from the rattled emcee.

"The song is—'Sapphire☆Phantasm'!"

She shouted in a clear, carrying voice. A voice that might have reached the top of a hill out in the country.

◆ Thus the nightmare strikes

After the program had ended without further incident, I was waiting for Saikawa in the TV station's underground parking garage.

"Damn, she's good."

While I waited, I'd been skimming social media comments about the program on my phone. The ones I saw were critical of the emcee, and most of them supported Saikawa.

Naturally, Saikawa's parents hadn't been cleared, and the prosecution would probably keep investigating. Still, Saikawa had taken the awkwardness in the studio and flipped it with just one song. No, she'd done better: she'd turned around the spite of the general public, which was a hell of a feat.

"It was like SIESTA said."

There had never been anything I could do. I'd only needed to watch Saikawa's decision play out. Witnessing that had been my job this time around.

Now all I had to do was take Saikawa back to SIESTA's house. Except...

"She sure is taking her time."

All she'd had to do was go to her dressing room, change, and come back, but I'd already been waiting for over half an hour.

"Hm?"

Come to think of it, I'd called for the car, but it wasn't here yet either.

Actually, it had been a while since I'd seen anybody at all. This underground parking garage wouldn't exactly be crowded...but still, in the last thirty minutes, not a single soul had passed by.

Then, I thought I felt a tepid breeze.

"...!"

On top of that, all the lights in the garage began to flicker. There were irregular spells of darkness, and then the lights went out completely.

"Gimme a break."

As I said, I'm bad with stuff like this. I took out my smartphone, using it as a flashlight. If I turned around now, *something* was *bound to be right there.* I'd seen enough paranormal shows to know how this worked. I backed up against a column, squinting into the surrounding darkness.

Now I had to make a phone call. If I was talking with somebody, no ghosts would show up. They'd covered that in *Shinken Zemi.* I punched in a number with a shaky fingertip. "C'mon, Natsunagi, pick up, Natsunagi, Natsunagi, Natsunagi Natsunagi Natsunagi Natsunagi Natsunagi Natsunagi Natsunagi Natsunagi." I called her over and over like a total stalker, but Natsunagi didn't answer.

This can't be because of the ghost too, could it? They mess with radio waves and stuff, right? Just when I was working myself into a panic—

"Oh? They're...on?"

They weren't as bright as they had been, but the lights had begun to glow, dimly.

...Geez. Don't scare me like that.

I stepped away from the pillar, ending the call.

However, I'd forgotten the fear I'd had earlier. If *something was going to show up,* it would be now, when I'd relaxed.

"What an opportune place to find prey."

The next instant, a sharp pain ran through the back of my neck.

"...!"

I couldn't even scream. The strength drained out of me, and I slumped to my knees.

I didn't understand what was going on, but a fear of death skittered around my mind—

"I suppose a tidbit will avert the crisis."

Still, if my premonition was wrong, it was only because *it* had detached itself from my neck sooner than I'd expected.

"…!"

Collapsing onto the asphalt, I looked up at the figure that had been standing behind me.

It was a tall man, dressed in white from head to toe. His hair was silver, his eyes golden. His face was very handsome, but cruel and haughty. His lips were stained with my red blood.

"Who are…?" I asked. My mind was hazy.

"What's wrong, human?"

Then *he spread two large, black wings.*

"Have you never seen a vampire before?"

◆ Mystery meets high fantasy

The blustering night wind woke me up.

…Woke me up?

I looked around. I was on the roof of some building… Probably the TV station.

And…

"You're awake, human?"

He was sitting cleverly on top of the narrow fence around the roof. He had one knee up, and he was holding a wineglass full of…something.

"What's the matter? Entranced by the sight of *your own blood…?*"

The silver-haired, golden-eyed man swirled the contents of the large glass. He was grinning boldly at me.

The nightmare wasn't over yet.

"How did we get up here?" I asked, feeling the wound on my neck.

"What a dull question." The man *drained the rest of my blood* in one gulp. "I held you to my breast and flew. Obviously." Once again, he spread those jet-black wings.

I'd been praying I'd seen wrong, but I'd have to admit it: This guy was not human. He was a vampire, a monster in human form found in folklore from all times and places. Their kind drank human blood and enjoyed eternal life. They were spoken of in legend as immortal kings.

Except...

"...I think someone might take that the wrong way. Could you not?"

This guy had already bitten my neck. I didn't want him talking about breasts or whatever on top of it.

"Have no fear. You need only to be still and offer yourself to me."

"You're doing this on purpose, right? You're deliberately making this weird."

"A noble vampire, and his human thrall. You know the rest, I trust?"

"I sure as hell don't! Are you calling me a sub?!" *Nobody said that. I need to calm down.* "Hey. Vampire. What the heck are—?"

"Scarlet." The vampire cut me off. "That is my name. The name of the king. Past, present, and forevermore. I command all nights, control the ignorant, unwashed masses."

It was a sharp change from the banter earlier. His golden eyes glowered, as if he were a huge snake that had spotted its prey. It made all my hair stand on end.

There was no point in trying to compete with this guy, or outwit him, or plot anything of the sort. I could tell even from a few meters away. No, *he was making me see it.* Vampire and human. Our level—our *rank*—as living beings was different.

"Ha! Be at ease, human."

Scarlet leaped down from the fence, his expression softening. He wasn't smiling, of course; his face and attitude were still insolent, but the threatening aura of a second ago had lost its edge. "There's no need to worry. I won't drink your blood again. I am interested only in beautiful people."

"Hold it. Did you just call me ugly?"

Even Siesta never said anything that mean to me, all right?

"Ha-ha. What's this, human?" The next moment, Scarlet had closed the distance between us and appeared right in front of me. He put that extremely handsome face close to mine, set a fingertip against my chin, and whispered sweetly. "—Do you desire my affection?"

"...Why am I suddenly seeing rainbows?"

"Sex and gender are trivial matters. Your values are out of date, human."

Who'd have thought I'd be getting that lecture from a vampire?

Scarlet snorted, instantly putting distance between us again.

"Wait a second. You're only interested in beautiful people, right? Then why did you take my blood?"

"Hm? Ah, I'd neglected to eat for about two weeks. Truly careless of me. I was merely staving off an emergency. Had you not been there, I would have starved to death."

"Hey, hold up, Scarlet. I saved your ass, and this is how you treat me?"

How could he act like such a big shot? Why was he still raking up his silver hair like he was a magazine cover model?

"Men's blood really is revolting. If I hadn't gone two weeks without sustenance, I would have vomited on the spot. Right on your face."

"You almost kill me, and then you tell me that?!"

If this guy had been a human like me, I would have been punching him right about now.

Yeah, if we were equals. But this guy was—

"Scarlet, you're a Tuner, aren't you?"

"Oh-ho." The silver-haired man narrowed his eyes.

So I was right. The Tuners were twelve people who'd been given the mission of protecting the world from anything that endangered it. In that group, Scarlet's role was—Vampire.

When SIESTA had told us about them, I'd never even dreamed that the vampire was a real one. But here he was, right in front of me. I had to admit it.

"I see. You know, then? *The Daydream* said she hadn't spoken to you about it."

The Daydream. That was probably Siesta.

"You know Siesta?"

"Hm? You're inquiring about my relationship with that woman? ...Let's see." Scarlet looked thoughtful all of a sudden.

What's this? Why doesn't he have a ready answer? All he has to do is say what sort of relationship they were in. Like casual acquaintances, say, or coworkers.

"Well, there's no need to inform you."

"...Wait. You're not going to say? Or is it that you can't say?"

"Ha! Awfully curious about the relations between a man and a woman. Vulgar creature, aren't you?"

"Did you just say 'relations between a man and woman'? Are you intentionally being suggestive?" *You've got to be kidding me... No, he totally is. He's lying. It's obviously a lie. At least I really want it to be. During those three years, Siesta and I dressed, ate, and lived together. I'd never picked up on so much as a hint of another man. It's all right, it's okay...*

"If suggestion is what you seek, the scent of that woman's shampoo was—"

"~~~~~~!"

"You're quite easy to read, human."

My hand was raised to him, and Scarlet snorted at me.

...I prayed fervently that I wasn't the first human in history to get teased by a vampire.

"Hah! Have no fear. My relationship with that woman was nothing like your baseless suspicions." As Scarlet spoke, there was a distant look in his eyes. "If she was a daydream, I was a nightmare. Day and night. We never mingled."

Siesta the ace detective and Scarlet the Vampire.

There did seem to be some deep connection there, something I wasn't aware of.

However...

"Then I'm even more confused. Why did you come to me?" If he was trying to avoid Siesta, and I'd been her assistant...

"There are several reasons. First, because I'd received a request."

A request—that word reminded me of Siesta.

"Well, in my case, I suppose it would be *a contract*. An equivalent trade where I grant a wish, and the other party pays me a commensurate price."

"A price... You mean money?"

"In some cases, yes. I will accept anything I find satisfactory. Money, rank, the finest blood—if they bring me something I will be content with, I will lend a hand to anyone. Even *the enemies of the world*."

He smiled. Even though as a Tuner, he should have been one of the good guys.

"...Then did you come to me because you'd made a contract with somebody? And the one who asked for the contract is the one who has business with me?"

"You're half correct. One of my reasons for coming here was indeed the party I've contracted with. However, they have no business with you."

"Huh? So you don't need me for anything?"

But he'd gone out of his way to make contact with me. He must have had business with someone in my circle who was nearby, which meant—

"Saikawa, huh?"

Even if that was true, though, what would this guy want with her?

And who the heck had made a contract with Scarlet?

"If we're talking about beings who serve vampires, there's really only one."

Suddenly, someone spoke over our heads.

The owner of the voice touched down beside Scarlet.

"Ha-ha. We meet again, huh, Watson."

He laughed the way he always did, wriggling the tentacle that had sprouted from his ear at me.

"Bat...!"

Trapped in the coils of that tentacle, I saw Yui Saikawa's wincing face.

◆ The primordial seed, the girl of the vessel

Bat was a former SPES officer, and Siesta and I had a fairly deep history with him.

We'd met him four years ago, on a plane at ten thousand meters. Siesta had defeated him then, and he'd been in the custody of the Japanese police ever since.

He'd broken out, though, and here he was. Right in front of me.

And in the tentacle that grew from his ear was—

"Kimi...zuka..." Saikawa looked to me for help, her expression agonized.

"...! Siesta said she was going to deal with you."

Yesterday, she'd gone out to do just that. Had he evaded her? ...Siesta? Really? No, more importantly—

"Give back Saikawa, Bat." I took my gun from its back holster.

"Ha-ha! You're one dangerous producer."

Bat seemed to have been using his augmented ears to listen in on our conversation. He smirked at me. "Eh, that's fine. She's weighing me down anyway."

To my surprise, he released Saikawa without a fight.

"Kimizuka!" Saikawa ran up to me, then ducked behind me to hide, clinging to my waist.

"Are you okay?"

"He said I was heavy! Shoot him dead! Now!"

"Great, you sound fine."

Patting Saikawa lightly on the head, I faced down the other two. A vampire and Bat—that was who we'd be fighting this time.

"Bat, why are you with Scarlet? Didn't you team up with Seed?"

Fingers tightening on my gun, I looked from Bat to Scarlet and back.

"Hey, c'mon, one question at a time." Bat gave his usual irritating laugh.

"The substance matters not. Bat, I will leave the explanations to you." Scarlet cracked his neck. "I only just awakened," he said, and then he melted into the shadows.

"Kimizuka, was that...?" Saikawa stared after him, wide-eyed.

"He says he's a vampire. It's hard to believe, though." Except he'd left proof on my neck.

"I see. Congrats on your graduation."

"...I don't want to 'graduate' with a dude."

Also, this wasn't the time.

"Bat, what's your connection to Scarlet?" I pointed my gun at him again.

"Originally, Seed asked Scarlet to bring me back," Bat said, revealing a further link. "Apparently, SPES is short-handed. I'd parted ways with Seed once, but he made contact with me through Scarlet."

Right, this guy had left SPES on bad terms, and that was what had triggered the hijacking incident, four years ago. However, Seed had gotten Scarlet to contact Bat, acting like that whole past was water under the bridge. Then Scarlet had broken through the strict security and taken Bat out of jail... Out of the *big house*, the one I'd visited.

"No way am I going back to SPES, though. Actually, *due to a certain reason*, my interests and Scarlet's matched up, so we're working together."

"So you connected with me and Saikawa and left Seed out of it? It's pretty late in the game for this; what do you need now? You helped us out during that sapphire incident, remember?"

When SPES had gone after Saikawa's left eye, we'd resolved the incident with an assist from Bat.

"But now you're after Saikawa? Why? Did you decide to take her left eye after all?"

Saikawa caught the cuff of my sleeve and squeezed it. Her sapphire eye was a memento of her parents, and to her, it was more important than life itself.

"Good guess, but I've mellowed out. I'm not planning anything that fancy," Bat muttered quietly. He gazed dully at Saikawa. "I'm just here to recruit you. Would you join me?"

""Huh?"" Saikawa and I said in unison. What the heck was this guy talking about?

"It's simple. I'm asking you to help me defeat SPES."

"...Is that why you didn't respond to Seed's summons?"

"Yup. Right now, I'm building up my forces. I've got my ears, and she's got her eye." Bat's cloudy eyes turned toward her. "So, Yui Saikawa. Come with me."

He was trying to pull Saikawa onto his team with some kinda weak logic.

"Do you think I'll hand her over that easily?"

"You heard him. Kimizuka is abnormally obsessed with me."

"Saikawa, I know you're trying to help, but you're really not."

Seriously, she never reads the room.

"You and the new girl detective are free to come along, Watson. Bottom line is, I need to be stronger—if I'm going to defeat that."

Bat's expression turned stern, and he brought up the name of the enemy leader who'd recently begun to move. "Why has Seed, and SPES, been so quiet over this past year? Have you thought about that?" he asked me.

During the year I'd spent in my tepid life, it was true that SPES hadn't tried to contact me in any way. I'd figured they just weren't interested in me, since I was only Siesta's shadow. But...

"Is there a particular reason behind it?"

"Let's go back in time a bit." Bat took a cigarette out of his breast pocket and lit it. "Several decades ago, the big guy flew to this planet as a seed. He wasn't able to adapt to its environment completely, though."

"...!"

This was new information. Seed's body wasn't built to live on this planet... Was that why he was so particular about his survival instincts?

"So Seed's been looking for a human vessel that will be able to survive on the surface."

"A vessel... He's planning to hijack someone else's body?"

Apparently he was trying to keep his own mind and powers, but he would switch them to another physical body.

"That's right. 'Vessel' sounds pretty simple, but it's not as if just any body will do. It has to be compatible with the seed, or Seed won't be able to move in."

"Compatible? —Don't tell me... That facility..."

"You put two and two together, huh?"

Natsunagi had said that human experiments had been a significant part of her time at the orphanage six years ago with her friends. That had all been—

"Was that all to create a compatible vessel for Seed?"

Little kids had been collected at that orphanage and subjected to experiments just for that?

"The experiments went even worse than he'd expected, though. Far too few of their specimens were able to withstand the seed."

That had also come up in Natsunagi's story. The "durable vessels" had been few and far between. Alicia had attempted the experiment, failed, and died.

"On top of that, most of the compatible cases still had side effects."

"Side effects? ...You mean like your eyes?"

Bat snorted, exhaling a plume of smoke. He was a former human who'd forcibly attached a seed to himself; in exchange for gaining power as SPES, he'd lost his sight.

"Right. The side effects take away some of the senses of humans, or even shorten their lives. Seed wanted a perfect vessel... And he finally found two candidates. They were—"

"Siesta and Hel, huh?"

Seed had said something to me last year: "If I side with either of them, the plan won't come together."

Meaning he'd made Siesta and Hel fight each other, intending to use the winner as his vessel. He'd been trying to narrow his options from two to one.

"However, Watson, you already know how that went."

"...Yeah. Although I only just remembered."

After Siesta and Hel's fight to the death, Siesta's vessel had been lost when her body died...while the other vessel held Hel, Natsunagi, and Siesta, and was already filled to capacity. If he'd tried to force it open, he probably would have broken it.

In other words, whatever it may have meant for us, Siesta's sacrifice had robbed Seed of both his intended vessels at a stroke.

"Well, Seed spent a year waiting for the day when those two would split once again. When that time came, he'd move into the body of the survivor."

"...But then it never did."

When Seed observed Siesta and Chameleon's fight on that cruise ship, he'd probably realized that Siesta had permanently attached herself to Natsunagi's body.

"That's the size of it. Of course, Seed hasn't been sitting on his hands for the past year. It's just that every time he tried to use his followers to start something, somebody prevented him from getting the results he wanted. And so he decided to go through Scarlet, who outranks him, and make his next move."

That was what SIESTA had told us about—Seed had lost his most promising candidate vessel and was looking for a new one. In order to qualify, the person would have to be able to use the power of the seed effectively, and they couldn't have developed any major side effects. If there was anyone like that near me, it was—

"Kimizuka..."

I felt a small tug on my sleeve.

Yeah, I know. I'd come up with my theory ages ago.

"Seed plans to make Yui Saikawa his vessel, huh?"

◆ The ugliest choice in the world

Seed was planning to use Saikawa as a vessel.

Several things hadn't made sense to me earlier, but they all started clicking into place once we had that theory.

For example, in London last year, Seed had taken Ms. Fuubi's shape and visited me, Siesta, and Natsunagi (in her Alicia appearance at the time). He'd told us to "search for the sapphire eye."

Back then, I hadn't known what "the sapphire eye" meant, but he'd probably been talking about Saikawa. So a year ago, Seed had already been trying to bring us into contact with Saikawa—and keep her near Siesta as *a backup vessel.* Then he'd meant to size up Saikawa indirectly *and try to cultivate her.*

However, Siesta's decision had postponed that, and it had been a year before we'd met Saikawa in person. We'd been brought together by the advance notice SPES had sent to announce its crime: "I will relieve you of a sapphire worth three billion yen." That incident might have been an attempt to complete Saikawa as a vessel by putting her in danger.

"...So you mean, after Siesta died, things have been going according to Seed's script anyway?"

Seed had observed both the sapphire incident and the showdown with Chameleon on that luxury cruise liner. We'd thought we'd solved the problem, but we'd been in the palm of his hand the whole time.

"Exactly. Now that his most promising candidates are gone, Seed's going after that girl for sure. We should take steps to prevent it."

Bat dropped his cigarette to the roof, then made another attempt to convince Saikawa to join the SPES suppression team. "Besides, that girl has a better reason than anyone to fight SPES." Grinding his cigarette out under his foot, Bat looked at Saikawa.

"I do...?" Saikawa didn't seem to know what he was talking about. She cocked her head.

"Oh, I see. They didn't tell you what went into getting that left eye of yours."

Bat gave a little nod, as if something had just clicked into place.

I'd heard that Saikawa's parents had given her that sapphire eye, since she'd been blind in her left eye from birth...

"Think about it. Yeah, they may have been rich, they may have loved their only daughter, but do you think anyone would pay billions of yen *for a false eye that was just a pretty rock?*"

"That's..." Saikawa froze up.

Don't tell me...

"Does it have some kind of secret Saikawa doesn't know about?" I asked.

"I only learned this the other day," Bat replied, "but soon after the sapphire girl was born, she developed a malignant tumor in her left eye."

Cancer of the eye. I hadn't heard of any cases of that before.

"It's a rare disease that mainly shows up in kids under five. This country has less than a hundred cases of it per year. If the disease progresses, it's treated by surgically extracting the eyeball, but even then, you couldn't call it a full cure."

That was when I finally saw where he was going with this.

They'd probably anticipated that Saikawa's disease wouldn't be cured by ordinary methods. Even so, her parents had wanted to heal their only daughter, *no matter what it took.*

"So Saikawa's parents turned to SPES?"

In order to save their daughter's life, they'd asked for help from a great evil.

"No..."

Saikawa's hands trembled at the revelation. Her parents hadn't told her. They probably hadn't wanted to make her anxious.

...No, that wasn't all of it. What they'd feared most was—guilt.

"They invested enormous sums in SPES's experimental facility," Bat said, and all the possibilities clicked into place.

When Natsunagi had told us about her past, she'd mentioned a wealthy Japanese couple who'd regularly made big donations to the orphanage. Could they have been Saikawa's parents?

And then there were those reports about Saikawa's parents and illegal accounting. Had they found the suspicious money stream from six years ago?

If all those theories were correct, then...

"...Just tell me one thing, please."

Saikawa let go of my sleeve. With effort, she spoke to Bat calmly. "If a normal person formed a contract and learned SPES's secret—once that contract came to an end, what would SPES *do with those people?*"

I knew what her question meant instantly.

Before I could stop him, though, Bat answered.

"They'd kill them."

This was the worst scenario I could think of: Saikawa's parents hadn't died in an accident. SPES had taken their lives.

"That can't... No..."

"Saikawa!"

Saikawa staggered, nearly falling, and I caught her from behind.

...Last night, Saikawa had told me she had next to no connection to either Siesta or to SPES, and so this was a story that belonged just to her. She'd taken pride in her own life.

But now they'd all linked together anyway.

She was right smack in the middle of this churning nightmare, and there was no way out.

"That means you have a reason to fight, Yui Saikawa. You're destined to take up arms against SPES." Bat drew the gun from his back and tossed it toward Saikawa.

He was wordlessly telling her to take it and fight.

"I'm…" Saikawa's voice was trembling.

Saikawa had only just learned everything—the truth behind her eye, and the truth of her parents' death. She was nowhere near capable of making any choices right now.

"Bat, now isn't—"

Just as I tried to take a step forward in her place…

"For hell's sake. Could you be any worse at this?"

A figure welled up from the shadows near Bat, and I recognized those golden eyes and silver hair.

It was Scarlet, the white-jacketed vampire, who'd just woken from his brief nap. He needled Bat irritably. "I'm appalled that you thought you could talk her around with that travesty of a negotiation, *mammal*. You stand down." Scarlet stepped out in front of Bat.

"Ha! Vampire. Don't get me wrong. I did ask for your help, but that doesn't mean I'm bad at…"

Just as Bat was about to snap at him—

"Don't push your luck—lower life-form."

Scarlet's gold eyes flickered like lightning.

"…!"

Suddenly, Bat fell to his knees. Then, as if he was moving against his will, he bowed to Scarlet.

"…Damn…it."

Bat was struggling, but his agonized face gradually slipped out of sight, until at last his head was pressed to the ground.

"I will not permit a mere human to disrespect me. Grovel there for a while and allow me to show you how this is done."

Was that another vampire power? After Scarlet had dominated Bat without even touching him, he turned to me and Saikawa again.

"Now, then. I am sorry for the trouble you've been caused."

Well, that was a surprise.

"No, we're…"

"He must understand that any attempt to form a contract must be accompanied by a commensurate price." Ignoring my confusion, Scarlet steered the conversation off in another direction—and it didn't take me long to realize it was the worst one possible. "What do you say, sapphire girl? Should you accept his request and assist him in subjugating SPES, I will grant you one wish."

"A wish…?"

When she heard Scarlet's proposal, Saikawa wavered.

"That's right. You can wish for anything you like. For example—"

The vampire whispered sweetly.

"—why don't I bring your parents back to life?"

◆ What we the living can do

"Bring Dad and Mom back to life…?"

Saikawa's right eye widened. It was as if she'd been offered a thread of possibility, a miracle she'd thought could never happen, and her heart swayed unsteadily. —But.

"That's not even possible." I knew it was cruel, but I cut that sweet hope down. "When someone dies, they never come back."

Everybody knew that.

The dead don't come back to life. What's gone never returns to the way it was. That's what makes us irreplaceable. We know this.

"Yes, you are not wrong." In a flat voice, Scarlet temporarily acknowledged what I was saying. But then… "However, I am a vampire—an *immortal* king. Remember?"

Still expressionless, the vampire bowed his head at a ninety-degree angle—and then he called toward hell.

"Return, lizard."

★   ★   ★

In the next instant, a human silhouette rose from Scarlet's shadow.

"Kimizuka, that's…" Even the half-distracted Saikawa stared in astonishment.

The figure was a slim man with silver hair and Asian features—and *a long, reptilian tongue.*

"Chameleon…"

He was a SPES officer, and our old enemy. We'd first encountered him in London a year ago, but at the end of that recent showdown on the cruise ship, he'd been lost in the ocean—or so I'd assumed.

"Why are you alive?"

Chameleon leaned forward limply, his long tongue hanging down. His shape was definitely the one I'd seen several times before in battle… But.

"—Ah, ah, aaaah, aaaaaah."

The sound seemed to echo from the depths of the earth.

"What the hell is this?"

Chameleon said nothing coherent, just kept making that awful noise. His eyes were unfocused, and he swayed on his feet in an anemic daze.

Was this really Chameleon?

"Put bluntly, he is what one would call a zombie." Scarlet shot a cold glance at Chameleon. "The immortal blood in my veins can resurrect the deceased as the undead."

"…! So he's a corpse puppet?"

Scarlet walked around the three of us, smiling coldly. "Corpse puppet. I see. Yes, that's good. It's true that he cannot speak, nor can we communicate with him. He has lost his sense of pain, and his remaining physical senses hardly function at all. In that sense, he really is no more than a living corpse. However…" Scarlet went on. "The undead I create by drinking blood return with their strongest *instinct* from life intact. Put another way, they can attain the *wishes* they harbored then. Well, human?" He turned to me.

"If you could have your wish granted even after death, would that not be happiness?"

Humans and vampires had completely different values—and that was what separated us. Either that, or this messed-up thought experiment was what happened when vampires tried to compromise their take on life and death with humans'.

I knew what this man was saying was wrong, but I didn't have an immediate response.

"Well? What will you do, sapphire girl?"

Scarlet's focus shifted from me to Saikawa. Well, she was the one he'd offered this choice to in the first place.

"Have no fear. I don't even need a corpse. If their bones, hair, or even DNA remains, I can resurrect your parents as undead."

"......" Saikawa said nothing.

A warped smile stole onto Scarlet's lips. "Go on," he murmured. "Decide quickly, or *the bystander* won't keep his silence."

Just then...

"—Ah, ah, aaaaaaaaaaaaaaaaaaaaaaaaaaaah!"

The shriek was deafening.

"Saikawa, look out!"

Chameleon had flung his upper body back and screamed. He wasn't conscious; he didn't even know why he was standing here. He just howled, as if it was all he could do. Unsteady feet tangling, he lurched toward us in an attempt to attack.

Chameleon's instinct was to fight for survival.

Even after he had died and come back to life, he kept up that meaningless struggle.

...Because that was his wish.

"That's not what you told me, vampire."

Just as I heard that voice, Chameleon stopped moving.

He'd been reaching out to grab us, his eyes rolled back into his skull... but there was a long tentacle wrapped around his body.

"Oh-ho. You managed to move. Impressive, Bat."

Still facing forward, Scarlet spoke to the man standing behind him. This was the first time he'd used Bat's name.

The tentacle from Bat's left ear had reached out and restrained Chameleon. He'd protected me and Saikawa.

"Hey, vampire. You didn't mention that your undead were this half-assed." Without flinching, Bat snapped at Scarlet again. "I proposed a contract because I thought you could bring the dead back to something that resembled actual life."

A contract with a vampire—that must have been the "interests matching up" that Bat had mentioned. He'd placed his hopes in Scarlet's ability to bring the dead back to life and had offered suitable payment. But the power hadn't been as almighty as he'd thought.

"Nonsense." Scarlet turned back, flatly dismissing Bat's challenge. "How could there be a miracle without a price? Nothing can be gained without sacrifice: That is a natural principle. Or, what, did you seriously suppose that *your younger sister could be brought back as you once knew her from a single hair?*"

"...! Shut up!" Bat was furious. He didn't turn that anger on Scarlet, though. Instead, he tightened the tentacle that bound Chameleon, taking out his frustration on the incomplete undead.

"—Ah, aaah, ah!"

Chameleon groaned in pain. He was no longer the enemy who'd given us so much trouble before.

"Come, sapphire girl. Choose." One more time, Scarlet offered the choice to Saikawa. "It is true that the revenants are degraded, but there's no need to fear. As I said before, the undead I create return with their strongest wish in life. Sapphire girl, what do you suppose your parents' instinct was?" Scarlet asked Saikawa, before narrowing his golden eyes and answering his own question firmly. "Love for their child, freely given. Therefore, once returned, even if your parents are reduced to corpse puppets, no doubt they'll never forget their love for their only daughter. Listen, sapphire girl," he said again. "Do you not wish to see them, one more time?"

Saikawa's only response as he made his case was silence. She stood very still, fists clenched tightly.

However, right in front of her...

"—Gah, ah! Aah!"

Even wrapped in Bat's tentacle, Chameleon kept wordlessly trying to attack us. Saikawa was standing beyond his outstretched hand. The gun Bat had thrown to her earlier lay at her feet.

"Saikawa..."

I started to say something to her—then changed my mind. This time, there was nothing I could do.

After all, before we came here, SIESTA had told me to watch over Yui Saikawa's decision. I had a hunch she'd meant this one as well.

"All right, girl. What will you do?"

Scarlet pressed her to make a decision.

Chameleon had dragged himself right up to her. Saikawa had to do something now; she finally bent down and—

"You poor thing."

Gently, she stroked Chameleon's head.

"......"

Scarlet said nothing. Saikawa watched him out of the corner of her eye...and didn't even glance at the gun by her feet. With a sad smile, she softly ran her hand over the groaning Chameleon's silver hair.

"You don't have to do this anymore. A kind ace detective and her assistant already put an end to your fight. It's all right now. Please rest."

...Of course. Chameleon had been created just to fight as Seed's clone. In a way, he was a victim. His struggle had ended with that showdown on the cruise ship. Siesta had seen to that.

"—Ah, ah, aaah." Chameleon howled, desperately wringing his voice from his throat. He might have been trying to tell us something. But the meaningless sounds only faded hollowly into the night sky.

"He's telling me to sing." Saikawa studied his face, as if she had managed to divine what he wanted.

"...Really?"

"I don't know."

"Hey."

Despite the weight of the situation, the retort just came naturally.

"Well, how could I? The dead don't tell us anything." Saikawa straightened up.

"Some people might say we're full of ourselves, but I think all we can do is consider what that person would want, believe in it, and carry it out."

Turning back, she smiled at me. That smile seemed fragile, and it was sadder than any expression I'd ever seen from her. The sincerest, too.
"—Yeah, you're right."
What did the dead want from those they'd left behind? There was no way to truly know. How did Saikawa's parents want their only daughter to live now? They'd never be able to tell us.
But Saikawa still believed.
She trusted that the path she'd chosen for herself was the future they'd wanted as well.
"I'd always like to be someone that Dad and Mom would be proud of if they were alive. I was a wallflower with no friends, but now I'm singing, surrounded by a crowd of fans and companions. I think that would make them both happy."
That was what Yui Saikawa believed to be her parents' last wish.
She wouldn't be tainted by revenge. She'd just enjoy her time with her friends and continue her career as an idol.
"So I'm sorry. I trust that this will make you happy as well."
As Saikawa spoke, I saw a mic in her hand—or imagined one, anyway.
This was her requiem for Chameleon, and for her parents.
And that was fine. That was how Yui Saikawa should be. Idol singers weren't meant to hold a gun.
Saikawa sang, whether or not the situation called for it, ignoring both the pseudohumans and the vampire.
"All right, please listen. The song is—"

She'd sing, and sing, and sing.

◆ That day's regrets, someday's promise

"I'm worn out..."

Later, back hunched and shoulders slumping, I trudged down the dark road that led back to the hideout.

"Kimizuka, I was gonna say you look like an old man, but you're more of a zombie now," Saikawa admonished me. She was walking beside me.

"We had a vampire, a pseudohuman, and a corpse puppet all in one place back there. Anybody would end up zombified."

"Ah-ha-ha! It was an all-star assembly, wasn't it?" Saikawa gave an easy laugh.

I almost told her, *Man, you don't have a care in the world, do you...* But it was a relief to see she could smile like that after everything.

"Seriously. I'm impressed we made it through."

I thought back to the exchange on the roof, about half an hour ago—

"Ha-ha, ha-ha-ha!"

Putting a hand to his forehead, Scarlet grinned broadly. He seemed to find this hilarious.

"What was that girl? One would think she no longer saw me at all."

In the end, Saikawa hadn't even given Scarlet's offer a response. She'd finished one song in her rooftop recital, then hurried back to her dressing room to change by herself.

From the way she was acting, though, her intentions were clear. Saikawa wouldn't bring her parents back to life. Chameleon's incomplete resurrection had been enough to show her that they wouldn't genuinely come back.

And even if her parents weren't here, Saikawa could get by on her own. That was what mattered. Her left eye would show her what lay ahead. This was her story, a life that was hers alone.

"The world has some very entertaining humans in it," Scarlet commented, approaching Chameleon's corpse.

After Saikawa had gone, I'd finished Chameleon off.

This was the second time I'd killed him. I knew it was a weird thing to say to an enemy, but I silently prayed that he'd rest in peace.

"By the way, Scarlet, why did you help Bat instead of Seed?"

Bat had disappeared into the darkness ages ago, so the vampire and I were alone. It seemed like a good time to ask.

"You could say it was a whim… However…" There was something oddly significant in Scarlet's tone. "I wished to *see the 'singularity' for myself.*"

What did he mean, singularity?

He peered at me. "Besides."

"?"

"The price Seed initially offered to pay me *was abnormal.*" Scarlet smiled thinly. "I thought it would be intriguing to go along with his caprice, so I accepted. Still, it led me to an encounter with something fascinating. Now, I shall take my leave."

Scarlet nimbly jumped up onto the fence.

"What exactly did Seed try to pay you?"

"Ha! Deduce it for yourself someday, human… If you are the man who stands beside the daydream, that is." Scarlet spoke over his shoulder to me. "Well, I suppose I'll ask a question of my own while I have the chance to."

Turning halfway around on his narrow perch, Scarlet said:

"Is there no one you wish to bring back to life?"

He looked down at me, his expression unreadable.

Bringing the dead back to life was profane. If it was really possible, then I'd—

"Well, you needn't answer now. In any event, this visit is merely my *debut.* My true entrance lies in the future. Find your way to it someday, human."

Then Scarlet leaned backward, letting himself fall.

When I saw that…

"It's Kimizuka. Kimihiko Kimizuka."

Even I don't know why I did it. Only that the next thing I knew, I'd given him my name.

★ ★ ★

"Kimizuka? …Kimizuka!"

Somebody tugged at my sleeve. I glanced over and found Saikawa looking up at me, perplexed.

"We're here."

"Oh, sorry. I was thinking."

While I was absorbed in the memory of that last exchange with Scarlet on the roof, we'd made it back to SIESTA's house.

"Honestly! You're the only one who'd let your mind wander while I'm talking to you!" Saikawa glowered at me, then turned away sulkily. Apparently, she'd been trying to strike up a conversation with me.

"Sorry." I patted her lightly on the head, but she was still pouting.

"Enough. I'm not talking to you anymore, Kimizuka."

"Well, that's just sad…"

Is this how dads feel when their daughter goes through a rebellious phase?

"I'm sorry." She'd smacked my hand away, and I lowered it with another apology.

Saikawa was striding ahead, without waiting for me. "I told you—"

"I'm sorry I couldn't do anything."

"Huh?" She turned around.

I really should have said all of this to her before I said anything else.

"I'm sorry I couldn't say anything to you. I'm sorry all I could do was watch. I'm sorry I couldn't help. All I could do was wait for you to get through it on your own, Saikawa, and—"

Just as I was about to finish the sentence, something caught me around the waist.

"I'm sorry," I said just one more time, and then I hugged Saikawa back. She'd flown into my arms.

"…Three years." I heard Saikawa's vaguely needy voice from a little ways below my chest. "It's been three years since anyone hugged me."

Three years. By now, I didn't even have to ask what that number meant to Saikawa.

I couldn't take her parents' place, though. Nobody could. Nobody could replace anyone.

Still, I thought. *Still*.

I could walk with her. I could hold her hand and pat her head. I could also hold her close like I was doing now. In that case—

"I'll let you cry on my shoulder anytime." I wanted to do for her what no one had done for me a year ago.

"You too, Kimizuka." Saikawa looked up at me. "You can lean on me and be more demanding too." It was clear from her expression that she wasn't joking. "It's okay to do what *you* want to do."

Saikawa had said this to me before.

True to her words, she'd chosen her own path. She was sure her deceased parents would be proud of her as she pursued her career as an idol singer, surrounded by friends. She also knew it was what she personally wanted to do.

Then what about me?

I'd inherited the deceased ace detective's last wish…but was that really what I wanted to do?

What exactly was it that my heart wanted right now?

◆ Everything changes now

"We're hoooome!"

Heading down the underground stairway, Saikawa opened the iron door.

It had been a long day, but we'd finally made it back to Siesta's hideout.

"Sorry we're laaaate," Saikawa called to Natsunagi and Charlie, who'd stayed here. After all that mess, the clock on the living room wall said it was past midnight.

"I'll just take a shower, then hit the sack." …Or so I thought, but first I probably needed to fill the other two in on what had happened to me and Saikawa. Especially the part about Seed's objective and what was going on with SPES, fast—

"Nagisa!" Saikawa shrieked. She was crouched down beside the dining table in the living room.

"What's wrong—?!"

Natsunagi was on the floor, unconscious.

"Nagisa! Nagisa…!" Saikawa called, then started to shake her roughly.

I stopped her, then put my hand by Natsunagi's lips to see whether she was breathing… Okay, she was alive. Then, while we were doing that—

"…Kimi…zuka? Yui…?" Natsunagi's eyes opened a little, and she registered me and Saikawa.

"Are you okay?!"

"Nagisa…!"

We'd crouched down beside her.

"R-run…," she croaked.

In the next instant, I could feel something deadly behind us.

"…!"

Snatching the gun from my waist, I turned and pointed it at the figure that was standing a few meters away. My opponent was pointing *a slender sword* at me.

"Why…?" Saikawa murmured in a tremulous voice when she saw the face of the person I was holding at gunpoint.

…Yeah. I knew how she felt. Even now that we'd taken aim at each other, I doubted my own brain. Maybe this was some sort of dream, or an illusion.

At the same time, I was well aware that *this person* wasn't the type to play practical jokes.

So as for me, I chose to keep my tone as light as I always did with her.

"Hey, c'mon. This is a pretty big personality shift—Charlotte Arisaka Anderson."

Between her flowing blond hair and emerald-green eyes, there was no mistaking her for anyone else. Just a day ago, we'd been close friends, living under the same roof. Now she was eyeing us coldly, as if we were prey she needed to hunt.

"Run for it," I urged, stepping in front of Natsunagi and Saikawa to shield them. But Natsunagi was in no shape to go anywhere under her own power, and Saikawa was frozen with shock.

"It's no use." Charlie's expression was heartless. "Even if I have to chase you to the ends of the earth—*I will kill Yui Saikawa.*"

Not Natsunagi, not me. Less than an hour after Saikawa had just freed herself from a powerful set of shackles, Charlie was declaring that she was the target she had to annihilate.

"Wh-why?" Saikawa sounded less shocked than genuinely perplexed. "We were together all day yesterday, and we chatted for so long..."

"I have orders," Charlie told her briefly. "They came in just a little while ago. And so I'll do it. There's no other reason."

Who would issue orders to kill Saikawa?

SPES? No, it couldn't be them. Bat had told us that SPES—well, Seed—was trying to take Saikawa over and use her as a vessel. He couldn't kill her.

"It's time." Without telling us anything else, Charlie leveled her saber. "If you get in my way, I'll kill you, too. I won't let you stall for time."

In the next instant, she'd vanished.

No—it only looked that way. That was how fast she'd closed the distance between us.

Charlie was taking this seriously. It wasn't like she even needed to; I'd never managed to beat her in combat, period. If we were in a one-on-one fight now, I was already—

"I knew I was right to drink your blood."

I'd heard that same mocking tone just a little while ago.

The vampire stepped between Charlie and me, golden eyes gleaming, as red drops of blood danced around him. He was in control now.

"...! Scarlet, you—!"

But that blood was his. Along with the bright blood, *Scarlet's right arm was tumbling through the air.* Charlie's sword had severed it.

"Oh-ho. To think you'd lop off my arm." The sudden intruder had startled Charlie; meanwhile, Scarlet didn't turn a hair. "My compliments. You're quite skilled...*for a human.*"

Catching his flying right arm in his teeth, Scarlet unleashed a high kick at her.

"...!"

But it was no ordinary kick—he was a monster, after all. There was a dull thud, and Charlie flew backward.

"Ghk! Who...are you...?" Charlie had crumpled to the floor a good distance away. She looked up at Scarlet in obvious agony.

"It appears you hadn't factored my existence into your plan." Scarlet pressed the arm against his bleeding right shoulder. The surfaces rapidly joined up again—he didn't even have to stitch them together.

"Scarlet, why are you here?"

He'd hinted that we'd probably meet again someday, but I hadn't expected to see him less than an hour later.

"Oh, I'd forgotten something." Walking up to me, Scarlet slipped something into the breast pocket of my jacket. "This is the *price* I was going to receive from that mammal. Since our contract has been annulled, I thought to return it to him, but he told me to give it to you instead."

"Bat did?"

The object was small and hard. What in the world...?

"It's a stone that would let me walk under the light of the sun. —Or so he claimed, but I couldn't say whether it's true. It was a truly appealing notion for a vampire, but..."

Right, vampires can only go out at night. Bat had gotten something that useful for Scarlet to pay him for returning the dead to life?

"And so, human, that concludes my errand. You've made extra work for me." After disrupting the situation as badly as possible, Scarlet prepared to make his exit. I turned to him.

"Hey, vampire. Would you take those two and run away?"

I asked him to get Natsunagi and Saikawa to safety.

"Is that a formal contract? If so, then—"

"The price is my blood," I said, shutting him down in advance. He'd already taken that blood when we first met. If *the guy who'd saved his life* was asking him for a favor, he'd probably listen.

"…I see. However." Scarlet narrowed his eyes. "Are you sure you don't want me to defeat that blond girl?" He gazed at Charlie, who was getting unsteadily to her feet.

"Yeah, that's fine. It would be hard to ask for too big a favor for *disgusting blood.*"

"Ha-ha! What an entertaining fellow you are."

Besides, I have to deck her at least once. "That means I'll take over here." As I spoke, my eyes were on the girl I could never seem to get along with or get rid of.

Scarlet turned on his heel. "Very well. I accept your request. Next time, come to me bearing a new price—Kimihiko Kimizuka."

Holding Natsunagi and Saikawa to his sides, Scarlet spread his black wings and flew from the room.

"Kimi…zuka…"

"Kimizuka…! I promise, we'll—!"

Natsunagi and Saikawa gazed at me, on the verge of tears.

Geez. Keep that up and you might make me think you like me. Gimme a break.

"All right. Now."

The three of them were out of sight in no time, and then only Charlie and I were left.

There was no way I could cut and run, not after I'd done all that posing.

"Are you ready?" I watched Charlie steadily. She'd retrieved her sword.

"…I should ask you the same thing."

"Oh yeah? Well, whichever."

Let's get started, here and now. We have a year's worth of fighting to catch up on.

5 years ago, Charlotte

"...Ngh, guh..."

I sat huddled against the wall inside an old, abandoned warehouse, sobbing.

"They're going to kill me..."

I knew what failing to complete a mission meant for an agent. I hadn't killed my target, and now my life was hanging by a thread.

"Why? Why did this happen...?"

All of this, every single thing, was...

"Come on, stop crying already."

...the fault of my target, the white-haired girl next to me, who was casually holding out a handkerchief.

"If it wasn't for you—!"

Yeah—she was the target I was supposed to kill.

Code name: Siesta.

It was my first real combat experience since I'd joined the organization, and I'd been so nervous I'd thought my heart would burst. Even so, I'd cornered her in this abandoned warehouse, and I'd shot her in the left side of the chest...or so I'd thought. However, for some reason, she wasn't even wounded, and the next thing I knew, she'd pinned me down instead. Then she'd made me *a certain offer*, and here we were.

"I don't mind if you cry and yell at me, but your face is a mess. Here, blow your nose."

...*She has no idea how I feel.* Irritated, I snatched the white handkerchief she was holding and blew my nose on it as hard as I could. "Accepting mercy from my enemy. This is humiliating..."

"Heh-heh. Well, you were up against the wrong person." Next to me, the enemy gave an elegant smile. She was gonna drive me crazy.

"...! Fine already! Just do whatever you want with me."

Now that I'd failed in my mission, the organization was bound to take me out anyway. Dying here would be better than that, but...

"...But I don't wanna dieeeee!"

I was still only twelve. There were all sorts of things I hadn't done yet. I wanted to wear trendy clothes and eat yummy food. Obviously I'd been prepared for a worst-case scenario in a job like this, but that didn't mean I wanted to die.

"I already told you." As I sat there hugging my knees, the white-haired girl made her offer again. "I'll make it seem as if I died here. That way your organization won't kill you."

"...What's in it for you?"

Having an enemy help me was totally mortifying...but if I took her up on it, I just might survive this. The paradox was making it hard to answer.

"Why are you doing this job?" my target asked me out of nowhere.

"...My parents." I hadn't found my answer yet, so I decided to go along with the conversation. "They've been soldiers and spies for ages. I don't see them much anymore, but I've always respected them. Their names and faces are never made public. Some people say they're horrible, awful people, and that the things they do are a crime against humanity. But they protect this world from *behind the scenes*. I'm proud of my parents...and of my job."

And I meant it. This was my calling.

I would protect this world according to my own philosophy.

"I see. You're like me, then."

As she spoke, my former target wasn't looking at me.

Come to think of it, I didn't know much about her. Many spies and assassins research their targets thoroughly. Actually, I thought most of them did. This time, though, I hadn't taken the risk. I didn't want to start caring about her too much to pull the trigger.

"I'm working toward a certain goal, too. That's why I can't let you kill me now."

"Oh."

"But if you're doing the same thing, you shouldn't die here."

"...And so you're rescuing me?"

If so, she was the biggest pushover ever. Helping the person who'd tried to kill her...

"Exactly. And after that, I'd like you to help me."

"Huh?"

"It's the terms of the deal. I'll save your life this time. In exchange, I'd like you to help me with my work once in a while. What do you think?" She leaned in to peek at my face, smiling.

"...That's not fair."

Instinctively, I knew she didn't actually need my help. She was just calling this an "exchange" so that I could accept her kindness freely.

She hadn't just won; she'd annihilated me in every way.

"...!"

The tears I'd been holding back spilled over again.

"Oh, honestly. I suppose I'd better...," she said. I think she just couldn't stand to watch me break down. "Let me give you some advice, so that you won't make the same mistake twice."

She reached into her dress, fumbled for something, then brought it out.

"It's so pretty..."

It was a pendant set with a blue jewel.

The pattern from the refracted rays of light showed it was completely flawless.

"This stone could take a hit from an artillery shell. I put it over my left breast, inside my bra. I have an acquaintance who's very good at making these things," she told me casually. "I'd heard you were a good shot, so I was sure you'd strike my heart accurately."

"Then you knew the whole time...?" I murmured. I'd gone clear past surprise to amazement.

"First-rate detectives resolve incidents before they even occur, you see."

The smile she gave me would have captivated anyone who saw it.

"...I'm no match for you."

I'm sure that was the moment it happened. When I realized I wanted this girl to be my teacher. When I knew I'd do anything for her. —And so.

"What should I do first—Ma'am?"

Ever since that day...
Her wish has been my wish, too.

Chapter 3

◆ Yesterday's friend is today's enemy

The fact that Charlotte Arisaka Anderson and I didn't get along was nothing new.

We'd first met more than three years ago. I'd been Siesta's assistant for about six months then, and I'd finally gotten used to this extraordinary life. Not that I was happy about it.

"Kimi, there's someone I want to introduce you to tomorrow."

When Siesta told me that, I got all paranoid that I'd be meeting her boyfriend, and I was all anxious when I went to bed that night... Well, not really anxious. Just moody.

The next day, Siesta introduced me to Charlotte Arisaka Anderson, a girl about my age. My memories of our first conversation are still vivid:

"Who is this girl with the crazy dark circles?"

"Who is this guy with the crazy dark circles?"

It was less a conversation than a name-calling competition, and we were both short on sleep. That day, Siesta said she needed more help with a mission than I could give her, so she'd called in Charlotte...but the fuss she put up was completely abnormal.

I didn't know the details, but Siesta had become her teacher for some reason, and ever since, Charlotte had considered herself Siesta's first apprentice... And then I'd shown up as her assistant. It must've been a pretty big shock.

To no one's surprise, Charlie and I completely blew the job that day. Siesta had told us to work together to capture a certain target, but our first meeting had gone terribly and torpedoed any chance we had at successful teamwork.

"*Charlotte! How long does it take to figure out you're standing on my foot?!*"

"*Oh, I'm sorry. I thought it was your face.*"

"*Then get off of it!*"

We kept fighting, and since we prioritized showing off over the whole "working together" part, the target got clean away.

After that, we met whenever Siesta needed it, which was often, and we fought every time. When Siesta died, our relationship broke off temporarily...but here we were again. As a matter of fact, the relationship might never have broken off in the first place.

After all—

"Kimizuka, you'll never get married. There's just no way."

Even now, three years after we'd met, Charlotte was grousing at me.

"Man, that's not fair."

About half an hour after I'd had Scarlet evacuate Natsunagi and Saikawa, Charlie was insulting me. We'd had a knock-down, drag-out fight, and now we were sprawled out next to each other on the floor of the half-demolished living room.

"Well, I mean, come on. What kind of jerk hits a delicate girl in this day and age?"

Ah. So she was annoyed that the punch I'd thrown at the end out of sheer stubbornness had hit home. If she was going to take that tack, though—

"My injuries are way worse, all right?" I retorted through the pain of the cuts in my mouth. I was all torn up.

Even if that attack from Scarlet had weakened Charlie, there was no way I could win a straight fight against her. It was a miracle I wasn't dead.

"Haaah, my energy is gone. Help me up." Charlie sounded apathetic, as if the hostility from just a minute ago had never been. She raised both arms limply toward the ceiling.

"What are you, Siesta?"

"...I did not want to know that you and Ma'am did things like this."

"It wasn't because I wanted to. I had no choice." If I hadn't done it, that nap-loving detective would never have gotten out of bed.

"Haaah. Well, whatever." Charlie got up. "Here." She held out a hand to my black-and-blue self.

"Is that coated with poison or something?"

"You seriously don't trust me, do you?" Charlie started to laugh it off, but then— "Well, you've got a point." With a self-mocking smile, she quietly withdrew her hand.

After forcing my aching body to get up on its own, I faced Charlie. "Except you weren't actually trying to kill me. Were you?"

Charlie didn't answer.

However, in the earlier confusion, she'd said it herself: Her objective was to kill Yui Saikawa. Natsunagi and I just happened to be on the scene.

Besides, it really didn't seem as if she'd been giving everything she had in our subsequent fight. That hinted that there was still time to talk this over.

"If you keep getting in my way, I'll show you no mercy either," Charlie responded, although she looked away as she said it.

"Charlotte, why are you trying to kill Saikawa? Weren't you two friends?"

Saikawa and Charlie had first met on that cruise, about ten days ago. It was true that they hadn't known each other long, but we'd been living under the same roof for the past few days. It didn't seem as if Charlie could actually hate Saikawa... So why?

"Friends? Who are you talking about?" With a humorless smile, Charlie gave a flat no. "I've never made one of those." There wasn't the slightest hint of confusion in her expression, and she didn't seem to be bluffing. She genuinely thought that. That was how she'd lived her life. "All I do is carry out the mission I'm given, as part of my organization. That's my job, and it's the only way I live. There's no room for a fuzzy concept like 'friends' in there."

Charlotte Arisaka Anderson was a lone agent who'd undergone military training for the exceptionally talented since she was small, and she had belonged to a series of organizations on her own. As far as she was concerned, orders from her organization were everything. She'd never dream of disobeying them.

"So you're telling me your organization ordered you to assassinate Saikawa?"

Charlie nodded wordlessly.

Assassinate Saikawa—the first thing those words made me think of was SPES. After the earlier sapphire incident, that was where my mind inevitably went. But—

"Charlie, you're not telling me you've got a connection to SPES, right?"

Earlier, Bat had told me that Seed's objective was to use Saikawa's body as a vessel. SPES wasn't trying to kill her. However, some organization had ordered Charlie to assassinate Saikawa. I couldn't reconcile those two facts.

"...Yes, that's right. I haven't sold you out and gone over to SPES. As a matter of fact," she said, "it's the other way around. Both I and the person who issued my orders want to destroy SPES, just like you do."

"In that case—"

"What's different is the lengths we're prepared to go to in order to do it." Charlie's eyes were cold. She wouldn't allow any compromises or bargaining. "You already get it, don't you? Right now, Seed's deteriorated to the point where he has to switch to another vessel. If we destroy that vessel, what do you suppose will happen to Seed?"

"...! If the person he's planning to take over is gone, then Seed will..."

Die.

We didn't even have to fight Seed himself. If we just destroyed that vessel...

If Yui Saikawa died, Seed wouldn't last much longer.

"...So you want to sacrifice Saikawa in order to take down Seed?"

"I told you. We're prepared to go to different lengths."

"Who's 'we'?" I said, still aching all over. "You'd better tell me that, at least. Listen, Charlie. If you're an agent who obeys orders without question, then tell me: Who's your boss? Who thought of this ridiculous idea?"

"It's me."

A flat, cold voice echoed in the room. It was enough to shut down my exasperation instantly. I turned toward the door, and...

"I ordered her to liquidate Yui Saikawa."

A redheaded lady detective who always looked good behind cigarette smoke was standing there.

◆ The enemy was there all along

"Ms. Fuubi?"

Someone who hadn't even been on my radar had just walked in, and my thoughts froze up for a second.

In the meantime, she ground out her cigarette under her foot, then stalked over to me. *What in the world is going on?* I was about to ask, but—

"Charlotte, why are you slacking off?"

Before I could, Ms. Fuubi decked Charlie.

Charlie crashed to the floor, then curled up with a pathetic moan.

"…! What the heck are you doing?!"

Ms. Fuubi ignored me. She went over to Charlie and hauled her up by her blond hair.

"Hey, Charlotte. I'm going to ask you one more time. What are you doing?"

"I'm r-really…sorry…"

"Huh? Look, I'm asking what you're doing. I told you to kill Yui Saikawa here, didn't I?" Ms. Fuubi pulled on Charlie's hair even harder.

"…! No, what are *you* doing?!" I couldn't just stand by and watch this; I got between them.

"Kimizuka, is this somebody you should be protecting?"

…Yeah, she had a point. Right now, Charlie was trying to kill one of my friends. But still. "She's not somebody you should be hitting either, Ms. Fuubi."

"…Huh. You've almost got a spine now."

She stepped away from me and Charlie, although probably not because I'd convinced her.

"Are you okay?" I turned to Charlie; she'd put a hand to her swollen cheek. She must have cut her mouth; there was blood leaking out of the corner.

"I don't need you worrying about me."

"If you can manage insults, you're fine." In that case, there was just one person here I should be focusing on. "Fuubi Kase. What are you?"

She had Charlie working for her, and she'd ordered Saikawa's death from the shadows. Who was she really?

It was a perfectly natural question, and in response, she said:

"I'm the Assassin."

She made no attempt to hide it.

"...You're another of the Tuners?"

"Oh, you know that word already, huh?"

"Up until just now, I believed you were a kind policewoman, you know."

"Ha! There's no way a regular lady detective could become an assistant police inspector at this age." *Fuubi* lit another cigarette, then exhaled a big puff of smoke. "'Police officer' is just my cover. My role as a Tuner is Assassin: I hide myself, deceive everybody, and kill the enemy. That's my job."

"...So this time, your 'enemy' is Saikawa?"

"No." Fuubi narrowed her eyes. "My target is SPES. That's all."

...That matched what Charlie had said.

"Then you're going to kill Saikawa as a way to defeat Seed?"

Saikawa could become the vessel that would revive Seed. They thought that killing her would mean indirectly killing him.

"That's the one. Seed went out of his way to make contact with Scarlet. Then Scarlet started acting sketchy. Now Bat has too. We need to assume we're out of time. That's why I sent that girl in, undercover... I never thought she'd be so useless."

Fuubi sneered cruelly down at Charlie.

"......"

Charlie looked away, biting her lip and probably ruing her own clumsiness.

"If I hadn't been tied up with that *robot*, I would have been able to give the order sooner. She screwed up my schedule, dammit."

So SIESTA had been at Fuubi's since yesterday, huh? She'd picked up on the fact that Fuubi was the one we needed to deal with, not Bat. Then she'd fought with her for over a day, keeping her pinned down.

"So, Charlotte. Where are they now? You'd better at least know that much," Fuubi pressed. There was a threatening undercurrent to her voice.

"...Heading for the airport, it looks like." Charlie was still shaky, but she got to her feet, using the table as a support.

Had she put a transmitter on Saikawa? They'd been living together; she'd probably had plenty of chances.

"I see. She is wealthy, after all. Is she planning to use a private jet? Well, that's fine. I'll have them lock down the airports right away. Let's go."

Fuubi turned on her heel, heading out of the house with Charlie.

"You think I'm just going to let you go?"

If they did, I was going to be seriously offended. Without waiting for them to answer, I pointed my gun at their backs.

—But.

"Obstruction of justice."

Right after I heard that voice, I was on the floor with the wind knocked out of me.

For a second I thought I'd been shot, but I hadn't heard a gun, and I wasn't bleeding.

Just one blow. She'd hit me once, on the chin. That was all.

But my body wouldn't move, and my vision was gradually tunneling.

Ignoring me, the two of them left the house.

"...Should've said 'illegal firearm' first."

And with that pointless rejoinder, I blacked out.

I don't know how long I was unconscious.

Out of nowhere, I thought I'd picked up a familiar scent. As if I was following it, I slowly opened my eyes.

Someone was standing there, holding out a hand to me.

"...Si...esta?"

Without thinking, I said that familiar six-letter word.

The figure gave a deep sigh. Then she glared down at me in a way that seemed impossible for a machine.

"Are you stupid, Kimihiko?"

◆ If you'll be my assistant

"You look pretty pathetic," SIESTA said as she helped me up, a little exasperated. "Not only that, but you've completely trashed my house. I'll be sending you a bill for the repairs later."

"...Geez. Not fair."

This place had been hit by a whole string of enemy attacks. She should be thanking me for having protected it.

"Actually, you look awful yourself."

It was probably because she'd fought with Fuubi before she came here. Her clothes were ripped in places, and the skin beneath had taken heavy damage as well.

"I didn't lose. I just made a temporary strategic retreat."

"You're as proud as the original Siesta."

"And I only tore the maid uniform reluctantly, to suit your preferences."

"You don't have to copy the way she set me up as a pervert."

Get a load of this android. It isn't just the way she looks; even her personality and the way she treats me are exactly like the original. Even though both Natsunagi and Saikawa have settled the score with their pasts, and I'm just about to move on from a few things myself... Seriously, gimme a break.

"Hey, what should I do?"

...That means if I slip up and ask her for help, well, there was no way around it. It's not my fault. It's society's fault. It's Siesta's fault. "You probably know already, but they've basically got us in checkmate."

Charlie's betrayal had come out of nowhere. If things went on like this, Saikawa was definitely going to get killed, and maybe Natsunagi would get killed trying to stop them. If Charlie got serious, there was no way I could win a fight with her, and we were also dealing with Fuubi. A Tuner.

Besides, if I chose to help Saikawa, I might end up indirectly helping Seed revive—basically selling out the entire world.

"Pathetic." SIESTA sighed again, as if she couldn't stand to watch me stress out. "Kimihiko, your nature practically makes the entire world your enemy in the first place."

"Wow, I'm way too deep. What kind of humongous sin did I commit in my previous life, huh?"

Hey, even I'm not picking a fight with the entire world on purpose, okay?

—Besides.

"Even if that's true, Siesta was there."

The entire world might have been my enemy, but she'd stayed with me. She'd been frustrated with me; she'd say, "Are you stupid, Kimi?" but she'd still taken my hand and fought alongside me.

While she was there, I hadn't been alone.

"As long as Siesta was around, that was all I needed," I muttered, remembering.

"...Kimihiko, do you know you're doing that?"

I realized that SIESTA seemed upset.

"Hm? Doing what?"

SIESTA only muttered something at a volume I couldn't quite catch: "...I wonder what stirred my maternal instincts—the discrepancy or the dejected expression."

At times like this, she was usually saying something unflattering about me, so it was probably wiser to pretend I hadn't noticed... Kind of a sucky adage to live by, though.

"Well, what are you going to do, Kimihiko?" SIESTA turned back toward me. "You're facing a comrade's betrayal. A friend in crisis. Multiple enemies who are far too big and powerful. And, ultimately, the possibility that you might make the world your enemy. What will you do?"

SIESTA's blue eyes were gazing straight at me. I really couldn't believe that gaze was fake. It was exactly like it had been on that day. She was leaving the choice to me.

Should I fail to save my friend, and save the world?

Should I save my friend, and turn the world against me?

The decision was too weighty for me to make. How could it not be?

I'd spent all of my eighteen years getting pulled into stuff.

Now, suddenly, the fate of the world was in my hands? How?

"You don't get dragged into things. You drag others in."

★ ★ ★

...Yeesh. If it was going to be like this, maybe Hel was onto something back then.

In that case, though...there was only one thing I needed to do.

Just one sentence I had to say.

If I was really about to become a key figure dragging the world into peril, then there was one person I needed to pull in first.

It didn't matter if she wasn't the real one. It was okay if it was just for now. —Even so.

"Siesta— Be my assistant."

I had no idea what my face looked like right then.

I just held out my left hand, wearing what I was pretty sure was an awkward smile.

"Very well. Come this way."

Siesta accepted, but she didn't take my hand. She just walked off, heading deeper into the house.

"...Hey, Siesta, I was pretty impressed with that one." *It's going to be really embarrassing if she just ignores it. I mean, c'mon.*

"We've used up too much time as it is. We need to hurry, or we won't catch up with those two."

"If you're going to be sensible, I've got no comebacks to make."

"Also, for some reason, your attempts to make this a touching scene are incredibly irritating."

"I wasn't trying. That's, like, the meanest thing you could have said after that." Even as I complained, I followed Siesta down a corridor, and then—

"A wall?"

At first glance, it looked like a dead end, but...

"Open sesame." Siesta chanted a spell that was way past its expiration date, and the wall rumbled and slid to one side, revealing a set of stairs.

"Let's go." Siesta started down the stairs.

"Weren't there any better spells?"

"The words of the spell don't matter. It's designed to recognize my voice."

I see. This was Siesta's hideout, all right.

"So if I screamed, for example, 'Kimihiko's first love was Siesta,' it would still open."

"You have no proof. And this isn't one of those security questions for when you forget your password."

"We're here."

At the bottom of the stairs was a vast open area, like an airplane hangar. A big motorcycle with vaguely familiar coloring sat inside it.

"It's the *Sirius Version Beta*." Siesta promptly climbed onto the white bike. "This is the vehicle mode of the humanoid weapon Sirius."

"That thing we rode in London?"

Right, Siesta had said she'd negotiated with the British government to borrow that. Now that I thought about it, that had only been possible because she was a Tuner and could formally negotiate with the army.

"But will we be able to catch up to them on this now?"

"We'll take a shortcut through the tunnels."

How far did this space go? *Don't tell me it goes all the way to the tunnels in London.* I was about to ask when my gaze shifted from the bike to Siesta.

"...When did you change clothes?"

She'd switched from the ragged maid outfit into the military dress the former ace detective had worn. "Quick-changes are a mandatory skill for detectives."

"I think they're more important for idol singers, really."

And also, don't just change in front of a guy like that's normal... Geez.

"All right, let's get going. Hold on tight."

"Yeah, yeah."

Prompted by Siesta, I straddled the bike and put my arms around her waist.

Pale silver hair and a gray dress. This was the back I'd seen constantly for three years.

"Please stop indulging in sentiment while hugging my waist."

"Haaah. Your body sure is nice and warm."

"That's the grossest thing you've ever said. Actually, Kimihiko, you're pretty free with sexual harassment, aren't you?"

"Because I'm constantly on the receiving end, yes. C'mon, once in a while is fine."

"Of course it isn't. Seriously." As SIESTA said that, *she smiled suddenly.*

"Listen, SIESTA. You wouldn't happen to be...?"

"All right. In that case, let's *go discipline the apprentice.*"

However, it only lasted for a moment. SIESTA's expression turned serious again, and...

"—Sirius, prepare for launch."

With that, she revved the engine.

"You didn't think that was cool, did you?"

"I'll shake you off."

◆ The detective is always right there

About fifteen minutes later...

"According to my calculations, we'll overtake our target in approximately six minutes and twenty seconds," SIESTA murmured to me over her shoulder. We'd left the underground tunnel and were riding down a coastal road. There were no other people or vehicles in sight.

"Once we catch up to them, we'll be dealing with the Assassin and an agent, huh?"

Of course we'd known that when we set off. Still, the thought of how tough the enemies up ahead were going to be made me tense. Especially Fuubi. As a Tuner, she'd be as powerful as Siesta and Scarlet.

"There's no need to get so worked up," SIESTA said, still gripping the handlebars. "All you'll have to do is fight alongside Charlotte, Kimihiko."

"? But Charlotte's the one we're fighting, right?"

"Well, that's true too, but..." SIESTA was being oddly evasive. Like the former ace detective, apparently this robot wouldn't just come out and tell me the important stuff.

"By the way, where's that thing you've always got?" Since I was holding on to SIESTA's waist, I'd noticed that something she ordinarily wore on her back wasn't there.

"Oh, that? I gave it to an acquaintance a little while ago."

"Just like that? Do you know how important Siesta's memento is?"

"She really seemed to want it, so I thought it might be all right."

"This acquaintance who 'really wanted' a musket is a pretty dangerous character, too." I dunno who she was, but that's not a friend I'd want.

"But do you have any ideas about how to beat those two when we don't even have a weapon?" I asked SIESTA, speaking over her shoulder.

"Hm? Not really, no."

"What, you don't?!"

She'd sounded so confident this whole time that I'd just assumed she had a plan...

"Only..."

"Only what?"

"You've got one, don't you, Kimihiko?" As she spoke, SIESTA didn't look back.

"Well, sort of." It was too clumsy to qualify as a strategy; it was more like a last-ditch Hail Mary. And so—

"It doesn't sound as though you're going to tell me about it."

And I didn't. Besides, although I couldn't pin down exactly why...

I had the feeling she'd stop me if I did.

A short while later...

"Kimihiko, over there."

A road on the cliff's edge, with the ocean visible below. A motorcycle was racing down the road ahead of us. SIESTA sped up, pulling closer, and then we could see familiar red and blond hair.

"Kimizuka..."

Charlie, who was riding in back, noticed us closing in behind them. "...Why did you come after us?" She narrowed her eyes slightly, her blond hair streaming in the night wind.

"The truth is, I wanted to see you again."

"Ugh, so pretentious. It's been a year and you still haven't gotten your driver's license?"

"Siesta, feel free to ram her."

"I was also wondering why you weren't driving, Kimihiko, since you're the man."

"Hey, I'm not sexist."

Even though it completely wasn't the time, we joked around with each other the way we always did. Meanwhile, our bike drew up alongside the other.

"What, that *robot* still isn't broken?" Fuubi glanced back, mocking us.

"Yes, I'm particularly good at playing dead." Siesta responded with a joke she'd picked up directly from the original.

"Ha! I guess I might as well make this into a car chase."

With a roar, Fuubi gunned her engine. Undaunted, Siesta sped up as well.

…Except just as our bike passed in front of a white lighthouse that stood on the cliff's edge…

"Do it."

On Fuubi's orders, Charlie turned back, took aim, and fired her gun.

"…!"

Siesta leaned to tilt the bike; I copied her, and we managed to evade.

"Now you've done it," Siesta muttered, a little aggressively. And then—

"Launch missile."

She pressed some sort of button near the bike's hand grip.

"…! Charlotte, bail!"

"Huh?"

The next instant, our motorcycle fired a small guided missile. The missile struck home, and it went up in flames. The blast rocked our motorcycle, too; we skidded out and went tumbling over the asphalt.

"That was overkill…!" Forcing my aching body to move, I grabbed the guardrail and pulled myself up.

"That's the Sirius Version Beta for you. Excellent firepower."

"Look, maybe she got us once, but even for payback that was ugly."

Flames were blazing out of control on the other side of the street. I could see Fuubi lying on the ground nearby. This hadn't actually solved the problem, had it? With that thought, I started to go closer, and that's when it happened.

"Kimihiko!"

A gunshot.

SIESTA had shoved me out of the way, protecting me from the bullet. From beyond the black smoke, the agent was closing in.

"...!"

As if she was cutting through the wind itself, Charlie slashed at us with her saber.

"I'll do it. Get back, Kimihiko."

Instead of her musket, SIESTA took a blade that looked like a rapier from some hidden recess of her dress and prepared to fight back.

"Charlotte Arisaka Anderson. I've heard you're extremely skilled with a gun. Are you sure this is how you want to fight?"

"Against you, this way is better." Charlie brandished her sword as if she knew bullets wouldn't work on SIESTA.

Under the lighthouse, out in the sea wind, the two struck at each other in a cacophony of metallic clangs, and the fight unfolded at a speed no normal human could process.

"...! First that vampire, now you. There really are a lot of irregulars around here," Charlie spat out irritably.

"Irregular? I'm not sure that's the best way to think about it."

"What, you're planning to lecture me? Now, when you're even dressed like Ma'am...!"

"No. I don't have that right. However, if this were Mistress Siesta..." As SIESTA spoke, she was facing down a blade that was larger and thicker than her own sword. "I don't believe she would have looked outside herself for reasons something hadn't gone her way."

As she delivered that sound argument, she struck back.

"...!" SIESTA's sword skills forced Charlie to put some distance between them. "...You always were like that." Charlie bit her lip and spoke in a strangled voice, as if she was remembering someone else through SIESTA. "I first met Ma'am five years ago. At the time, I wasn't working under Fuubi Kase yet, and a certain organization had ordered me—to assassinate Siesta."

This was something I hadn't known about Charlie and Siesta. I had heard that she'd met Siesta before I had, but I'd never asked them for details.

"I obeyed my orders and tried to kill her...but it didn't work. I'd failed in my mission. Do you know what that means for an agent?" Charlie's question wasn't directed at anyone in particular.

If I were going to answer...I would have said that an agent who failed to carry out an operation would be killed by their organization. Especially if they'd botched an assassination.

"I knew what my fate would be. If my target didn't kill me in retaliation, the organization certainly wouldn't forgive my mistake. I thought my brief life was over. But..." Charlie hung her head. "As I started to lose hope, she told me, 'I'll make it look as though I died here, so you'll be all right.' I was her enemy, but Ma'am protected me."

...Yeah, that sounds like Siesta.

Sometimes she'd just decide to protect people, to save them, independently of her role as a detective. It was as if she thought of everyone besides herself as a client.

"She said, 'In exchange, I want you to help me out with jobs once in a while.' To seal our contract, she gave me this blue pendant." Charlie squeezed the pendant that always hung around her neck.

Siesta had probably asked for Charlie's help in order to protect her. Siesta was a Tuner, and if Charlie was affiliated with her, nobody but the best of the best would have been able to touch her.

"Ma'am was always like that. She protected me. Even when she died last year, she'd already made arrangements for me to start working under another Tuner immediately. It was as if she'd known it was going to happen."

"...And that Tuner was Fuubi Kase?"

Charlie didn't deny it.

Even after death, Siesta was sheltering her.

"That hasn't changed. Even as an android, you haven't changed a bit." Charlie's voice was trembling slightly.

It wasn't because she was crying, though.

"You're still holding back when you fight so you won't kill me!" When she raised her head, her face was suffused with anger.

"Why?!" Tightening her grip on her saber, Charlie rushed at Siesta.

"Why are you holding back?! Why won't you get serious?! Why are you still— Why are you trying to protect me again?!"

As Siesta parried Charlie's ridiculously fast swordplay, her cool expression didn't flicker. She didn't strike back any more than she had to, though. She stayed on the defensive.

"A year ago, I was so helpless. And so I swore…this time, I'd take SPES down in Ma'am's place. No matter what kind of unfair things happened to me under that other Tuner, I promised I'd be the one to avenge Ma'am… And yet—" She took an aggressive step in. "I can't even beat you, and you're just a machine! Why?!"

Charlie swung her sword to the side. However…

"Your movements are hardly efficient. When you get emotional, you can't exert even half your true strength." Bending backward, Siesta evaded the blade. Then, in an economical motion, she swung her rapier and knocked Charlie's weapon out of her hands, sending it behind her.

"…! In that case!"

In the next instant, Charlie's eyes were on me.

"I'll do anything to win."

She drew her gun from the small of her back, taking aim at me.

"Kimihiko!"

Staying low, Siesta got between me and Charlie and sent the gun flying with her rapier. But—

"I knew it. You really can't kill me." Somewhere in there, a second gun had appeared in Charlie's left hand. "It's over."

"……"

Siesta was on her knees. The muzzle of Charlie's gun was pointed at her forehead.

The situation was dire. Even Siesta couldn't turn this one around.

And if that was how things stood…

"Charlie, can you really shoot?"

I hadn't been any use at all so far, so it was probably about time I did something.

"What do you mean? Do you think I'd hesitate after every—"

"Even if *that's the real Siesta's body*?"

◆ That's why her will won't ever die

"The real...Ma'am...?"

When Charlie heard that, she stopped moving.

Her mind seemed to be racing. As she stared at SIESTA, her eyes were both steady and uncertain.

"You'd figured it out?" The first one to move in that deadlocked situation was SIESTA. "Kimihiko, when did you notice?"

She was still on her knees, and she didn't turn to look at me as she spoke. From the way she phrased the question, though, she'd already admitted that my guess was correct.   .

"I'm not sure when it was. The things that tipped me off were really vague, though."

If they pressed me for a clear reason, I didn't have one to give.

It might have been the familiar scent I'd had near me for three years, or the warmth of her skin when we happened to touch. It could have been the thought that no mechanical doll could give a sudden, hundred-million-watt smile like that. In other words, I'd had the contradictory hunch that, *some way, somehow, this was absolutely Siesta.*

"You're correct," SIESTA told me quietly.

I knew it. She really was the ace detective I'd spent those three years with, through good times and bad. However, her mind had stayed in her heart, and that had gone to Natsunagi. Only this body, her physical shell, was Siesta's.

"After that final battle with Hel, Mistress Siesta's body was frozen," SIESTA told us quietly. "It was what she had wanted. In accordance with a promise they'd made in advance, *a certain individual* put it in cryostorage. Then, using Mistress Siesta's vast knowledge and memories as a database, they loaded an artificial intelligence into her brain and spinal cord, then equipped the body with an artificial heart. That is how I was born."

"...So that's what happened..." All I could do was nod.

Even after death, Siesta found a way to be revived as an android and watched for an opportunity to contact us. She'd done it in order to pass the memories of last year's tragedy onto us and to help us wipe out SPES.

"Somehow I thought that might be what it was," Charlie said. "I didn't spend as much time with Ma'am as Kimizuka did, but even I remember her scent."

Come to think of it, Charlie had sniffed a lot of pillows when we were living in the hideout. Had she picked up on the faint, lingering traces of Siesta?

"—Still," she went on. "So what? Even if your body is Ma'am's, that doesn't change my mission. I'll defeat SPES in her place."

Charlie's gun was still pointed at SIESTA's forehead. However, a single tear trickled from her blazing eyes. "I mean, look. Nagisa could never kill Yui. That means *I have to do it.* By defeating Seed, I'll carry out Ma'am's last wish—"

The muzzle of her gun was trembling slightly, as if to match the quiver in her voice.

I see. Yeah, Charlie, you really were that type of girl.

She'd said she didn't need friends, and yet she'd continued to make Siesta her top priority... Then, somewhere along the way, Siesta's influence had pulled her to protect other people.

She was trying to carry out Siesta's last wish, trying to keep Natsunagi from getting her hands dirty, and really worrying about Saikawa, her target. The disconnect between her mission and what she felt was messing her up to the point where she was even looking to me, her sworn enemy, for support.

Geez. She was as clumsy as ever. She hadn't changed a bit since our first meeting. She was just like she had been for those two and a half years, when we'd fought so much we got sick of it.

Our stubborn bond had rotted to the point of snapping, but somehow it was still here. Sighing, I turned to Charlie just one more time. "Are you sure you're okay with that?"

"...! What do you know, anyway? You spent all that time just spacing out."

"Yeah, you're right. I'm sorry about that."

The fact that I'd been missing memories was no excuse. After Siesta's

death, I'd spent a full year soaking in lukewarm water, savoring a coun-
terfeit peace, and I really couldn't talk.

But... I said them anyway.

Her last words.

"The legacy Siesta left was me, Natsunagi, Saikawa, and you, Charlie.
All four of us. If you want to carry out Siesta's last wish—Saikawa can't
die."

It wasn't just Saikawa, of course.

We couldn't lose me or Natsunagi or Charlie either. Not a single one
of us.

"...! But Ma'am is a Tuner. Her mission is to defeat SPES!"

Yeah, that's right. As the ace detective, Siesta had fought threats to the
world. There was no doubt about that.

But.

"Charlie. Would the teacher you loved have prioritized protecting her
mission, or her friends?"

"...!" Charlie's face crumpled.

"Do you really think defeating SPES by sacrificing Saikawa is how
Siesta wants this to end?"

"Shut up...!"

Charlie yanked the pendant from her neck, snapping the chain. It was
almost like a symbolic gesture to help her look away from the past, and
from Siesta. She flung the pendant to the ground—but the charm popped
open, exposing the photograph inside.

"...Why is she smiling like that?"

The photo showed Charlie and Siesta, and they were both smiling. It
was as if they had no missions, nothing tying them down. It was a peaceful photo, something they might have taken to post online on their way
home from school.

"This is, this is just—!"

Charlie shook her head. Acknowledging Siesta's smile would put her
current mission on shaky ground. It would mean denying Siesta's last
wish, the one she'd believed in all this time.

And so, as if she was saying goodbye to the past and to Siesta, Charlie brought her foot down on the pendant.

"...!"

Or tried to.

Before she could do it, SIESTA slid her right hand in between Charlie's foot and the ground.

"...Ow."

"Oh— I'm sor...ry..."

SIESTA's objection was so calm that Charlie apologized on reflex. SIESTA picked up the pendant, put her hands around Charlie's neck, and tied the broken chain back together.

"Why...?" Charlie stared at her, dumbfounded.

Turning to face her again, Siesta sighed. "I swear..." Then she said it.

"Are you stupid?"

It was a phrase only the former ace detective had been allowed to say.

Of course she wasn't here, in SIESTA.

Her mind was with her heart, in Natsunagi.

Even so.

Her body, or her brain, or her mouth, must have remembered those words. For three years, she'd said them practically every day, and now SIESTA had just—

"That's the first time." Charlie lowered her head, as if she was struggling to contain some emotion. For a few seconds, she seemed to be thinking about it, and then— "That's the first time you ever said those words to me."

When Charlie raised her head again, her tearful face was radiant. She looked like an apprentice who'd always longed for her teacher to get angry at her.

As she watched Charlie, SIESTA's expression softened into a wry smile. She spread her arms, and just as Charlie was about to dive into them—

"Charlotte. This is why I keep telling you you're simple."

★   ★   ★

What connected with Siesta's chest was not Charlie, but a bullet.

"…!"

"Ma'am!"

Siesta crumpled where she stood, and Charlie caught her in her arms. Beyond them stood the Assassin—Fuubi Kase.

◆ The golden blade that takes revenge on the world

Gun in hand, Fuubi looked down on us from a short distance away. Her eyes were as cold as ice.

"I thought you had a little more sense than that, Charlotte. I guess you're no different from that brat over there."

"…!" Charlie gave Fuubi a sharp glare, then promptly returned her gaze to Siesta. "Ma'am…"

Dark blood was flowing steadily from the wound in the left side of Siesta's chest. Charlie ripped some fabric from her own clothes and tried to use it to stanch the flow.

"…Really, Charlotte, are you stupid?" Weakly, Siesta took Charlie's hand. "I'm not your 'Ma'am.'" She smiled faintly. Somewhere along the way, her tone had reverted to the one Siesta used.

"Never mind this. The person you two should be dealing with is over there." With a trembling hand, Siesta pointed at the one standing beyond us.

"But if it keeps…"

"It's fine. Emergency shutdown measures will be enough to deal with this." Siesta smiled again. I didn't know whether she was lying or not, but for now we'd just have to believe her.

"—We'll be right back."

Exchanging small nods, Charlie and I gently carried Siesta over to the guardrail. Then we turned to face our greatest enemy.

"Ha! Look at you two. You were just pretending you didn't get along, and now you're trying to team up?" Fuubi sneered. She stuck a cigarette between her lips and lit it, shielding it from the wind with one hand.

"You're really sure about this, Charlie?" I checked in with Charlie, without taking my eyes off Fuubi. "You've got a lot to lose if you go against her."

Due to her job, Charlie had made enemies of all sorts of people and organizations. Fuubi was the Tuner who'd picked her up after Siesta; without her support, Charlie's current position would be majorly threatened. There might even be more attempts on her life.

Most of all, she was voluntarily taking a stand against the mission she'd always believed in. Even if I was the one who'd talked her into it, I had to make sure this wouldn't be too much.

"It's pretty late for that." Charlie spoke firmly; she didn't look at me either. "Forget me, what about you? Are you prepared for this?"

"Of course. If running for it would work, I'd love to."

"...You call that 'prepared'? Are you sure you're speaking proper Japanese? Intelligence was the only thing you had going for you, right?" Charlie put a hand to her chin.

Don't worry about it. The fear's just scrambled my brain a little, that's all.

"Hey, Charlie, I just had a great idea about the fight we're headed into."

"That's our resident brain, all right. What strategy did you come up with?"

"If we survive this, let's get married."

"Huh? Ew, no."

"No, no, that was a reverse death flag."

"I'm not so sure about that concept."

"Before you head into a life-or-death crisis, you make a wish you'd never want to come true. Then you end up living and get what you asked for. It's an exploit."

"Our resident brain is an idiot." Next to me, Charlie clutched at her head.

Sorry. At this point, no brain could be much use.

"But..." Charlie raised her head and looked at me. "Apparently we've matured enough to attempt to compromise and work together, at least." She smiled, and I was sure she was remembering our first disastrous attempt at teamwork.

"Are you done with your strategy meeting?" Fuubi exhaled a big puff of smoke.

She'd waited for us... Nah, probably not. She'd just wanted to have that cigarette. And now our time was up.

"We'll catch her between us! Charlie, you go in from the right!"

"Okay!"

Charlie and I split up, aiming our guns at our target from two angles. Fuubi was grinding her cigarette butt under her toe. *Sorry, but we can't afford to wait for you to be ready.*

I leveled my gun, turning it on Charlie, who was right in front of me—

"...Why am I seeing Charlie?"

Charlie was looking back at me, eyes round.

Fuubi had been between us. Where had she gone?

"So you didn't have a plan, huh?"

Right after we heard that voice—

"...!"

First, I couldn't breathe.

Then I heard the sound of something sinking into bone.

The pain came a few seconds later, after I'd rolled several meters over the ground.

"Aaaaaaaaaaaaaaaaaaah...!"

The shock and pain made me scream pathetically.

I didn't even know what she'd done to me. Had she punched me? Kneed me? Something might already be broken. The pain was so bad I almost passed out.

"One down."

Promptly losing interest, Fuubi turned her back on me.

"...!"

Charlie pointed her gun at the other woman, warily putting a little more distance between them. While she was doing that, I managed to drag myself out of the way to the road's shoulder.

"What next? You're on your own now." Charlie's gun didn't seem to concern Fuubi. "Are you going to keep up this pointless resistance and delay the resolution of the problem?"

"……" Charlie listened to her, face stern, gun still leveled.

"Listen, Charlotte. I'm going to ask you one more time: What is your job? Weren't you going to take up the ace detective's last wish? Don't you care what happens to the world?"

"…I do care. I just can't believe doing things this way would make Ma'am happy."

"Ha! Are you crazy? It doesn't matter whether it makes her happy," Fuubi scoffed. "Can you save the world with ideals? No. All we have to do is kill Yui Saikawa, and there you go. World saved."

"I'm sure Ma'am wouldn't want to save the world by sacrificing somebody."

"Oh really? If sacrificing herself would do the trick, I'm pretty sure she'd do it in a heartbeat."

"What do you mean…?" Charlie's eyebrows drew together, as if she didn't know where Fuubi was going with this.

"Don't you get it? Here, let's review. Originally, Seed considered people who had a seed and could make full use of its power candidate vessels."

"Ma'am and Hel…"

"Right. But the ace detective's clever scheme shut that plan down. *She lost her ability to be a vessel by throwing her own life away.*"

Fuubi's theory went like this: A year ago, Siesta had chosen to die. She'd said she'd done it to protect Natsunagi and make her wish come true… but there was another reason she'd kept hidden. In her final job as ace detective, Siesta had put together a plan to defeat Seed.

"Then you mean Ma'am had picked up on Seed's true objective, and so she…"

Siesta probably hadn't told Charlie everything either. When she heard the deeper truth behind Siesta's self-sacrifice, her gaze wavered uncertainly.

"That's right. In order to protect the world, the ace detective sacrificed herself without a second thought. And remember what she said? You four are her final legacy. Know what that means? —She's telling you, *You take up my last wish and die for the world's sake, too.*"

"…!" That interpretation of Siesta's final words made Charlie's eyes go wide.

"Charlotte, you're brilliant. Don't let that lousy excuse for an assistant fool you. You need to understand the real meaning of the ace detective's last words and carry out her will."

"I..."

"Frankly, Nagisa Natsunagi isn't gonna cut it. She's too weak. That means there's nobody but you, Charlotte. You take up her legacy and become the ace detective, a Tuner." Fuubi's expression suddenly softened. "It's fine. If you're nervous, I'll train you again. You just carry out your mission. Kill Saikawa, defeat Seed. If you do that, you'll be the ace detective in both name and deed. Lucky you." Fuubi stroked Charlie's hair. "That was always your dream, right? Now it'll come true."

"The ace detective? Me...?"

"That's right. So let's go do that last job." With that, Fuubi turned her back and went over to the motorcycle SIESTA and I had ridden here. She was planning to use it to go after Saikawa and the others.

—But.

"What are you trying to pull, Charlotte?" Fuubi spoke without turning around.

She could probably tell without looking, just from the aura of hostility: Charlotte had her sword leveled at her back.

"Don't you want to be the ace detective?"

"...No. That was never my ambition." Charlie closed her eyes. Maybe she was reminding herself—or maybe she was finally facing her true feelings.

Thinking of the girl who'd been her teacher for five years, she squeezed the blue pendant that hung around her neck and shouted.

"Siesta was a beautiful, strong woman! *She* was what I wanted to be!"

Tightening her grip on her saber, Charlie slashed at Fuubi's back.

"Boring." Fuubi still hadn't turned around, but she dodged the attack lightly, without glancing at it.

"...!"

"You're selling me short. Did you really think you could beat me one-on-one?" Before she'd even finished the sentence, Fuubi drew her gun from her back and pointed it at Charlie's forehead. "Playtime's over."

Charlie's sword didn't quite reach her, and she was forced to her knees. Fuubi wouldn't hesitate to pull the trigger now. It also didn't look as if Charlie had any chance of turning the tables on her own. We'd been completely checkmated.

"You're right. On my own, I can't beat you." Charlie openly acknowledged her own defeat...or so it seemed. "But we haven't lost yet."

She looked up at Fuubi with blazing eyes, and in the next moment—

"Shift right nine millimeters and down seven— Now, Nagisa!"

With a noise that reverberated in my stomach, a shot was fired from high altitude.

"—!"

The bullet streaked out of the dark sky, knocking the gun from Fuubi's hand. And the person who'd fired it—

"That's one of Siesta's Seven Tools, all right. It's not shaky at all."

A familiar musket was protruding from the open window of the cockpit of a small fighter jet.

"...Well, look at that. You actually came back on your own."

Fuubi glared up at the fighter jet in the dark sky. "I guess that means you're ready for this—Yui Saikawa and Nagisa Natsunagi."

◆ That was the final answer

"Yui, Nagisa..."

Charlie looked up at the fighter jet flying near the lighthouse. It was a two-seater; Saikawa was in the pilot's seat, and Natsunagi sat behind her.

"I heard you'd gone to the airport. So you went to get that?" As Fuubi gazed up at the sky, she looked thoroughly unamused. She rolled her neck, cracking it. "First you pilot a small boat, and now it's a fighter jet. Compulsory education covers a heck of a lot these days."

"Any well-rounded young lady should be at least this capable... Or so I'd like to tell you, but it's almost entirely on autopilot. *A certain someone with very good ears* is piloting it remotely, relying on my eye."

Saikawa responded lightly to Fuubi's sarcasm. Apparently that quasi-pseudohuman was keeping an eye on our fight from some distant location.

"Ha! Are you two planning to side with this girl? She tried to kill you both, remember?" Fuubi snorted at Saikawa and Natsunagi.

"...!" Charlie bit her lip. She understood the weight of what she'd tried to do better than anyone.

But Saikawa said... "Yes, I'll save her. After all, she's my friend."

Someone had tried to kill her, and she was still calling them a friend. She went on, speaking directly to a very stunned Charlie. "Then after that, we'll have the fight to end all fights. You don't mind, do you, Charlie?" Saikawa grinned down at her.

"For your information, you won't just be fighting Yui," Natsunagi said from the rear seat. Her expression was prim.

Oh, right. Earlier, Charlie had hit Natsunagi with a devastating attack, too.

Natsunagi's voice was dripping with sarcasm. "Got that? When we fight, *we'll double-kill you*: once for me, and once for Yui."

Down on the ground, Charlie heard her out. "...Bring it anytime." Her eyes were just a little damp, but she was smiling.

"Relax. That future's never going to come."

A cold voice. The Assassin sprinted through the dark, bent on destroying the future Charlotte wanted.

"...!" Tightening her grip on her saber, Charlie faced down her incoming enemy.

Fuubi's gun had been shot out of her hand, and she was using a short survival knife now. Naturally, Charlie's weapon had a better reach, but Fuubi's skill far exceeded hers. Fuubi's outlandish moves forced Charlie onto the defensive, and then—

"Too slow."

—exploiting a vulnerability, she snapped the iron sword with a spin-kick, then knocked Charlie backward.

"...!"

There was a dull thud, and Charlie rolled across the asphalt. Immediately, Fuubi leaped to close the distance.

"Nagisa, do it!"

Just then, an airborne sniper targeted Fuubi. Saikawa used her eye to issue accurate directions; with her help, Natsunagi aimed the musket without hesitation and fired. "Sorry, but I can't afford warning shots." She kept firing at Fuubi; they'd brought the plane down a little to make it easier for her.

"You're in the way," Fuubi muttered, evading the bullets that struck the ground at her feet. And then...

"Huh?" Looking up, Natsunagi saw—a red-haired assassin leaping into the night sky. She'd caught the plane with a grappling hook and was holding on to a rope that hung from it. Fuubi jumped onto the cockpit, and then—

"...!"

She flipped her knife in a reverse grip and took aim at the startled Saikawa.

"No you don't!"

From behind Saikawa, Natsunagi fired at Fuubi. The bullet pierced her right shoulder, and the woman staggered back. —However ...

"Pain? You'll need a little more than that to keep me from fulfilling my mission." Fuubi's expression didn't change even as she fell from the plane, and she threw her knife into one of the engines on top of the main wings. There was a terrible *grunch* and a scorched smell. Black smoke billowed up, the plane listed to the left, and then they lost control.

"...! Nagisa, hold on to something!" Saikawa gripped the control stick desperately, but the jet kept losing altitude until it scraped across the asphalt in an emergency landing. The ground jolted upward as if an earthquake had hit, knocking me off my feet.

"...Yui..."

"Na...gisa..."

Natsunagi and Saikawa had gotten banged up pretty badly in the landing. They were obviously in pain, but the plane was in danger of exploding, and they managed to crawl out.

"So you finally came down here." Fuubi started toward the two girls, her movements smooth and menacing. Dark blood was streaming from the Assassin's right shoulder, but she still launched herself powerfully off the ground.

"—I can't have you forgetting about me yet." A figure cut in between them. "I told you, remember? I'm not alone. That's what lets me commit myself to my job."

"Charlotte, huh? But I've already destroyed your weapon."

In the black smoke, Fuubi pivoted on her right leg and raised her left leg high. But then—

"I'll borrow your help too." The smoke cleared, and there was Charlie, holding Siesta's rapier.

"…!" Fuubi couldn't stop. Her left leg swung toward the sword Charlie had thrust out, but—

"Kkha, hah…"

The agonized cry had been Charlie's. Fuubi had kicked her again, knocking her back several meters.

"Charlie!" Saikawa dragged herself toward the other girl. "Are…are you all…right?"

"…Ghk. Yes… But one of my legs is out of commission now."

Charlie had gotten the wind knocked out of her, but even so, she managed a smile. "This is how I… How *we* do things. Even if we can't win on our own, if we all combine our strength…"

"You're still playing friends? This is so pointless." Fuubi sneered.

"It's not…pointless…!" Natsunagi spread her arms. She stood as if to shield Saikawa and Charlie, who was on her knees. "We are…the final hope Siesta left. None of us will lose, and we won't give up. We'll all…win together…!"

Fuubi spoke quietly, either to her, or maybe to Saikawa, or to Charlie. "What…are you people?"

Her red hair had come loose, streaming in the night wind.

"You talk about companions, bonds, friendship, feelings, love, ties, connections—a last wish. What good is any of that to the world?" Fuubi's voice grew rougher and angrier. "Yui Saikawa: Your death will save the world. Charlotte Arisaka Anderson: If you kill Yui Saikawa, you'll save the world. Nagisa Natsunagi: If you were as strong as the former ace detective, you would save the world. So why don't you do it? What, you can't? Oh, well, I understand everything now. So just—!" Like the blazing flames, Fuubi screamed, her face filled with rage. "If you can't do that! If you're helpless…! Then at least be ashamed of yourselves. Don't sabotage the people who are fighting to save it!"

That scream might have been the first time I'd ever heard her say what she really felt.

"You're right." After a short silence, Natsunagi murmured, "I think what you're saying is probably correct. You're more right than I am, anyway. I'm sure there are people who would call that justice."

"If you understand that, then—"

"But," Natsunagi interrupted Fuubi. "The detective was too right, and she died." Justice didn't necessarily win. "So I want to choose something I know might be wrong. Even if it isn't correct, even if justice doesn't win, even then—I want to choose a future where the people who are precious to me are smiling next to me."

I don't want to let anyone else die.

Natsunagi flat-out rejected Fuubi, and maybe Siesta as well.

"Then we'll never see eye-to-eye."

I was sure Fuubi's fury hadn't cooled—but she seemed to have given up on changing her mind. "That makes this easy. The last one standing wins."

It was the simplest conclusion, and the most brutal one.

…But that was the only method left.

Actually, I don't think talking was ever an option here.

"Evil, meet your doom."

The Assassin ran like the wind. Soundlessly, so fast you couldn't even see her, she went to ensure justice was done.

"Nagisa!"

"Nagisa—!"

Natsunagi was still standing in the way, arms spread wide. Behind her, Charlie and Saikawa screamed.

"It's all right. Even if I can't see her, she's definitely watching me. She can hear my voice, too. Meaning—that ability will work."

Then Nagisa Natsunagi's *red eyes glowed.*

★ ★ ★

"Fuubi Kase, *you can't take a single step from that spot.*"

Fuubi stopped dead.

"…!"

She stood petrified, her eyes wide with astonishment.

Just one more step—her knife had frozen just before it plunged into Natsunagi's chest.

Natsunagi's red eyes were using the mind control. When she talked to Hel, then accepted her, she'd become able to use that ability.

"…! This isn't…enough to—!"

However, the Assassin wouldn't stop until she'd destroyed her target.

"Don't think you can stop me with an ability you just picked up!" Slowly, bit by bit, breaking down the mind control through sheer force of will, the knife descended toward Natsunagi. "Don't think nobodies like you three can stop me by yourse…"

Fuubi's eyes were wild with rage—but suddenly, her face went blank.

"Wait a second… 'You three'? The robot's out of the picture, but how long have I been fighting just the three of you?"

Realizing she'd missed something, she spoke to her targets without really thinking it through.

"Hey, where is he? *Where has Kimihiko Kimizuka been for the past few minutes?*"

It definitely wasn't arrogance. It was an accurate self-assessment.

Earlier, she'd disabled the powerless, lousy excuse for an assistant with one attack. She had me outclassed in every way. Even if I'd eventually recovered, as long as she could see me, she'd be able to deal with me. On that note, Fuubi had focused exclusively on Charlotte, and on the newcomers, Natsunagi and Saikawa. Her decision hadn't been a mistake.

Except for one thing.

If she'd made just one miscalculation, it was that…

"Kimihiko Kimizuka—*you swallowed Chameleon's seed, didn't you!*"

*   *   *

...the risk in gaining a pseudohuman power hadn't scared me one bit.

"I don't give a damn about side effects. You can take my senses or some years off my life, as much as you want of whatever you like. I'll let you eat it all," I told the seed of the parasitic plant that had settled inside me. Meanwhile, I made myself invisible and raced up to Fuubi. Right now, all I wanted was to KO that disgusting police officer. She'd twisted my beloved partner's justice, and as long as I could hit her for it, that was enough.

Are you sure it's enough?
I felt as if someone, somewhere, had whispered those words to me.

It's fine. It's not like I'm causing trouble for anybody, I told the speaker, clenching my fist.

I mean, it's true, isn't it?
"This is my story."
Then I punched the justice of this world in the face and sent it flying.

Epilogue

"You've got serious guts, arresting a police officer."

Fuubi's right cheek was red and swollen. One of her wrists was hand-cuffed, with the other cuff fastened to one of the guardrail posts. I had the feeling she wouldn't have put up a fight at this point anyway...but just in case.

"Still, I can't believe you actually swallowed that seed." Fuubi gazed up at me, looking rather appalled.

Chameleon's seed granted the ability to turn invisible. After I'd taken that first heavy blow from Fuubi, I'd used it to erase myself from the battlefield.

"You're gonna die."

Fuubi was watching me, her eyes narrowed.

"Yeah, I know."

Since I hadn't taken any precautions, I'd already known I'd be running that risk. That was why I hadn't wanted to use this plan if I could help it.

The seed was what Scarlet had given me at SIESTA's house. He'd extracted it from Chameleon's body when he'd temporarily resurrected him.

"Well, if my body breaks, it breaks." I might lose my sight, the way Bat had. It could even shorten my life... But. "I never was more than her shadow, so this ability's a perfect fit for me." I'd keep on being a behind-the-scenes kind of guy, as an assistant to somebody or other.

"Is that right? Fine. You hurry up and get over there too, then." Fuubi jerked her chin toward SIESTA.

SIESTA was lying by the side of the road, surrounded by Natsunagi and the others. Charlie had given her first aid, but she'd been shot through the left side of her chest. This woman was the one who'd done it, and she was still telling me to go to her.

"You're still Ms. Fuubi after all."

"What are you talking about? I'm your enemy."

"...Sure."

I had several questions, but I turned my back without asking any of them.

First off: Siesta, the ace detective, was the one in charge of subjugating SPES. Why had Ms. Fuubi helped out with that job after Siesta died, when she held a different position?

And another thing: the fact that SIESTA existed. She'd said that Siesta's corpse had been frozen to prevent decay, then fitted with an artificial intelligence and reborn as a mechanical doll. Who had acted so quickly?

If the person in question wasn't talking about it, I couldn't ask.

If she couldn't say, then I had to respect that.

Turning my back on Ms. Fuubi, I went to SIESTA.

SIESTA's eyes were closed. Natsunagi and the other two were watching over her.

"Ma'am." Charlie knelt, taking SIESTA's hand.

As if in response, her eyes opened slightly. "...As I told you, Charlotte, I'm not her."

"...!"

Charlotte was startled, and the robot squeezed her hand weakly.

"SIESTA!"

"Are you okay?!"

Saikawa and Natsunagi hastily called to her. She looked at them, and—

"Heh-heh." She smiled, her shoulders shaking slightly. "Honestly. You people are as noisy as ever." Slowly, with Charlie's help, SIESTA sat up. "I can't take a nice long nap if you're going to be like this." She cracked a special joke that no one else could get away with.

"SIESTA, you're all right?" I tried to check on her wound—but SIESTA shook her head.

"I've more than accomplished my mission," she said with another quiet smile.

"What do you mean?" Charlie gazed at SIESTA uncertainly.

"I'm no more than a program Mistress Siesta made to help settle her unfinished business."

"Ma'am's unfinished business?" Charlie tilted her head as if she had no idea what that might be.

"That's right. Mistress Siesta's legacy was the fact that she'd left the four of you—Kimihiko Kimizuka, Nagisa Natsunagi, Yui Saikawa, and Charlotte Arisaka Anderson—here in this world. However, each of you had *tasks you still needed to overcome.*"

Tasks left to the four of us. True, over these past few days, it did feel as if we'd confronted an insane number of problems.

"Nagisa Natsunagi had to learn who she really was, then face her past. Yui Saikawa had to accept the truth of her parents' death and choose how to live her life. Charlotte Arisaka Anderson needed to free herself from the spell of her mission and find a will of her own. And Kimihiko Kimizuka—"

After gazing at the others in turn, SIESTA looked at me.

"You had to move on from Mistress Siesta."

She astutely pointed out something I'd been pretending not to see.

"Mistress Siesta's only worry, the one thing that troubled her, was the question of whether you would be able to solve these heavy, painful issues. That was why she made me."

"...So that was, in the truest sense, Siesta's final job," I murmured.

SIESTA nodded quietly. "After all, her job was to protect the client's interests. To protect her companions." She quoted a phrase the ace detective always used to say. "Essentially, I was a maid who helped her in that endeavor."

"Then I was right? The problems that kept cropping up over the past few days were all..."

"Yes. They were tasks to help the four of you overcome the issues you harbored." SIESTA grinned like a little kid who'd pulled off a successful prank.

She'd encouraged Natsunagi to talk with Hel, opening the path for her to become the ace detective.

She'd forced Saikawa to confront a painful truth but had me stay with her as a friend.

She'd blocked Charlotte's path like a wall but helped her find something really important.

And she'd had me *assist* the other three in solving their problems so that I'd be able to accompany someone who wasn't Siesta as their *assistant*.

It was as if she'd predicted not just what we'd do, but Seed, Scarlet, and Fuubi. On top of that, she seemed to have used them to help us grow. Ordinarily, it would have been an impossible feat.

"First-rate detectives resolve incidents before they even occur, you see."

Another of the ace detective's signature phrases. SIESTA smiled as if she was rather proud of herself. "And so my role is at an end," she said with some relief.

"But… I'm still not…!" Charlie hadn't said all she wanted to say to SIESTA, and she wouldn't let her go to sleep.

"No, this is the end." SIESTA squeezed her hand gently, speaking softly. "I've completed my tasks. Mistress Siesta no longer has any regrets. The four of you will be able to live on and thrive. And so," she said, "smile and say good-bye to me."

SIESTA smiled at us. Her expression was a lot more nuanced than it had been when we first met her.

"I…see," I responded briefly.

This had been Siesta's final job: to help us, the legacy she'd left behind, to conquer our remaining problems. For Natsunagi, the past. For Saikawa, the truth. For Charlie, her mission. For me—the dead.

We'd all faced these things—and just now, we'd graduated. From the past, from the truth, from the mission, from the dead. And SIESTA, who'd helped us do it, had finally completed her job.

That meant you could probably call this a happy ending for all of us: Natsunagi, Saikawa, Charlie, me…and SIESTA.

Every one of us had accomplished something we'd needed to do. As a result, this was a beautiful place to end the story. It had to be.

Now, once SIESTA said her good-byes to each of us, we'd reach the moving climax. On that note, as the other three sniffled, I asked...

"In that case, did Siesta get a happy ending?"

It's like I said before:

It's still too soon for an epilogue.

The girls' dialogue

It happened about ten days ago. In the ruined casino on the sinking cruise ship, after the battle with Chameleon...

"I apologize for the delay," I said to the girl's back. Her shoulders flinched.

"...It's you, hm?" The black-haired girl turned to look at me. A little of her hair was tied up on the side with a red ribbon. She was sitting on the floor, and a sleeping boy in a suit jacket was resting his head on her lap.

"It's been a very long time, Mistress Siesta." She didn't look the same anymore due to certain circumstances, but this was *the mistress who had created me*.

"By the way, what were you just about to do?"

"What do you mean?" Mistress Siesta looked away from me pointedly.

"It seemed as if you were leaning closer to that boy's face."

"...I don't know what you're talking about."

"Nagisa will be angry with you."

"—Look, I told you, I don't know what you're talking about."

My mistress is completely adorable.

"Still, this is strange. I'm right in front of me." Shifting the boy to the floor, Mistress Siesta got to her feet and studied me.

To tell the truth, I currently have the exact same face as the real Mistress Siesta. I am a living android who's borrowed her body.

"That maid outfit looks good on you. I'm sure my assistant would fall for you in a heartbeat."

"? That isn't something I particularly want. Mistress Siesta, could it be that you want—"

"Now, about why I had you come here today."

Yes, my mistress really is adorable.

"I have another request regarding the plan we discussed." Then Mistress Siesta told me why she'd summoned me.

It was a certain program that she had left behind. A plan to transplant part of her memories and abilities into me, then further develop the four people who would carry out her last will.

"There's just one small change. I'd like to add this." Mistress Siesta held an IC chip out to me. "It's data about a mistake I once made."

"...? It's unusual for you to make mistakes, Mistress Siesta."

"...You're right. Apparently I really wasn't good at reading human emotions." Mistress Siesta smiled wryly. "And so, for the specifics, I'd like you to install that and look over the contents. There are new instructions on it as well."

"Understood, Mistress." That was how Mistress Siesta worked. She never told you everything on her own. I would go over this carefully later.

"Now my job really is over, isn't it?" As Mistress Siesta murmured, her face seemed somehow radiant. She sat down right where she was and began gazing at the sleeping boy's face again.

Yes, this was Mistress Siesta's final job, the one thing she'd said was still troubling her: watching over and raising *the four who were her legacy*. She'd entrusted that job to me, and now she would truly go to sleep.

I looked at her. She'd accomplished everything, her expression was peaceful, and—

"Mistress Siesta, a moment ago, you said you didn't understand human emotions. Do you understand your own?"

Mistress Siesta was still looking at the boy. Her shoulders flinched again.

"You... Just...do what I've told you to do." That was all she said. She spoke without turning around.

"Very well." I was only a maid, there to help and serve my mistress. I bowed, turned, and left.

However, for just a moment, a thought skimmed through my mind.

If it is a maid's duty to wish for her mistress's happiness, then what should I actually do next?

Prologue

"In that case, did Siesta get a happy ending?"

Siesta's eyes widen slightly.

But I mean, it's a good question, isn't it?

Say Natsunagi and I, and Saikawa, and Charlie, had all moved on from our pasts and spells and things like that.

Well, what about Siesta?

Had she managed to get a genuine happy ending?

"Kimihiko... That isn't right." Although her body was weak and unsteady, Siesta pushed herself to her feet. Natsunagi hastily put an arm around her shoulders, supporting her. "Mistress Siesta is satisfied with this ending. She's left the four of you as her legacy and has resolved your problems. That means her job is—"

"No!" I shook my head, rejecting the answer she was trying to give me. "Because, I mean...she was crying."

I thought back to the showdown with Hel at SPES's island hideout, a year ago. Siesta had chosen to seal the enemy by sacrificing herself, and our time together had ended. The pollen from that biological weapon had knocked me out, and I hadn't even been able to see her through her final moments.

But I remembered. Now, I remembered.

She'd been... Siesta had been crying.

She'd remembered how apple pie had tasted when she ate it with me. She'd reminisced about the time we lived in that cheap apartment. She'd looked back fondly on that photo we'd taken, with her in that wedding dress. She should have been with me the next day, and a week from then, a month from then, forever and always, and she hadn't wanted us to part.

She'd thought of those dazzling three years, and—

"Siesta cried and said she hadn't wanted to die."

And so, that's right. This has to be...

"Listen, SIESTA. When you kidnapped us and showed us those things from last year... That part at the end. When you showed us that final scene, where Siesta cried, after I'd collapsed from the pollen. Weren't you the one who decided to do that?"

After all, that stubborn ace detective almost never let people see her real smile. I couldn't believe she'd let me see her cry that easily. In other words, I'd seen it because the maid *had betrayed her mistress.*

So why had she done it? It had to be because—

"That's the real answer to your hunt for the mistake, isn't it?"

Natsunagi and the others looked startled.

That was the first problem SIESTA had set for me and Natsunagi: We were supposed to find a certain mistake Siesta had made a year ago. We'd found the one about Hel.

However, I was sure that hadn't been the only one. There had been another mistake, one even Siesta hadn't noticed.

That was why SIESTA had filed a *request* with me... Well, with Natsunagi, the ace detective. She'd asked the new detective to correct Siesta's mistake.

As a matter of fact, Natsunagi had already arrived at that answer herself.

She'd screamed it during the fight with Fuubi—Siesta shouldn't have died. The correct future was the one that found her smiling with the people she loved.

That meant that an ending where Siesta had to cry was—wrong.

"Kimihiko... What do you intend to do?"

In the curve of Natsunagi's supporting arm, SIESTA looked stunned.

I caught her by the shoulders and *shouted through her, to the girl beyond her.*

"Listen up!
I'm not giving up on you!
Even if you're satisfied with this ending, I'm not having any of it!
Sure, maybe nobody will understand!
Not Natsunagi!
Not Saikawa!
Not Charlotte!
Maybe it goes against everything in natural law!
But I promise you this—
Someday, I'll bring you back to life!
I'll do it, I swear I will!"

The next moment, Saikawa and Charlie latched on to my arms.
"You're such a dummy, Kimizuka."
"You're stupid, Kimizuka."
They were both crying as they held me up, big tears rolling down their cheeks.
When I glanced up, Natsunagi was gazing at me with a smile that was close to tears.
"You're so dumb, Kimizuka."
She'd set a trembling hand over the left side of her chest.
Had it gotten through to her?
Had my voice reached the other one who had to be in there?
"Honestly."
I heard a small sigh. Then, with a smile as if she was looking at kids who were a real handful, SIESTA said…

"Are you stupid? All of you."

I was sure she was saying it in Siesta's place.

A tear rolled down her face, and no one who saw it could have said she was a machine.

"...The sun's rising," she murmured quietly, looking to the side.

Dawn was breaking on the coast road. Orange mingled with the deep blue of the sky. Out on the ocean beyond the white lighthouse, night came to an end, and the sun peeked over the distant horizon.

"Yeah. This is where it begins."

Starting here and now, we'd rebel against our world.

The detective is already dead?

—No.

This is the long, long, dizzying story of the time until I take the detective back.

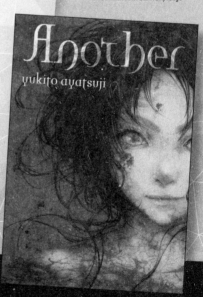

Our Last CRUSADE *or the rise of a* New World

LIGHT NOVEL

MANGA

LOVE IS A BATTLEFIELD

When a princess and a knight from rival nations
fall in love, will they find a way to end a war
or remain star-crossed lovers forever...?

AVAILABLE NOW
WHEREVER BOOKS
ARE SOLD

For more informatio
visit www.yenpress.cor